"There are things you need to learn, Emily."

"Is that the reason you kissed me?" she said quietly.

"Yes. No. Dammit, Em—" Jake drew a ragged breath. "Look, I can help you. I can teach you about men. What they want from women. The male-female thing, the thing you don't seem to understand at all."

Emily stared at Jake. He was right. He could teach her. He already had.

"Is that what you want to do?" she said huskily.

It seemed a long time before Jake answered. When he did, his voice sounded low and far away, even to his own ears.

"Yes. Yes, I do. And I promise you, Em, I'll teach you all you need to know."

Presents™

Passion™

Looking for sophisticated stories that **sizzle**?
Wanting a read that has a little extra **spice**?

Pick up a Presents *Passion*™—
where **seduction** is *guaranteed!*

Coming in April:
All Night Long
by **Anne Mather**
Harlequin Presents® #2170

Sandra Marton loves to hear from
her readers. Write to her (SASE) at
P.O. Box 295, Storrs, Connecticut 06268, U.S.A.

Sandra Marton

THE BEDROOM BUSINESS

Passion™

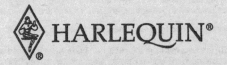

HARLEQUIN®

TORONTO • NEW YORK • LONDON
AMSTERDAM • PARIS • SYDNEY • HAMBURG
STOCKHOLM • ATHENS • TOKYO • MILAN • MADRID
PRAGUE • WARSAW • BUDAPEST • AUCKLAND

ISBN 0-373-12159-8

THE BEDROOM BUSINESS

First North American Publication 2001.

Visit us at www.eHarlequin.com

Printed in U.S.A.

CHAPTER ONE

JAKE MCBRIDE was a man under siege.

A woman who'd spent the past couple of months on his arm and in his bed, couldn't accept the fact that their relationship was over.

"You don't love me," she'd wept, just last night.

Well, no. Jake didn't. He'd told her that days ago, reminded her that he'd never said he loved her, never even hinted that he might love her someday. He knew there were guys who said it in an attempt to score, but he wasn't one of them. Jake was always honest about his intentions. He made it clear that love, marriage, the "something old, something new, something blue" thing just wasn't on his agenda.

Besides, the immodest truth was that he didn't have to.

He was a healthy, heterosexual, thirty-year-old American male. He was six foot three with broad shoulders, a deep chest and a hard, flat belly, thanks to his passion for tough, sweaty workouts at his gym. His hair was dark, thick and wavy; his eyes were what one besotted female had called the color of the Atlantic in midsummer, which even now made him smile because he hardly ever noticed his eyes—what man would?—except when he happened to see them in the mirror while he shaved. He had a square jaw and a firm mouth set beneath a nose that bore a small bump, a souvenir of the year he'd spent working a jackhammer in a Pennsylvania coal mine.

He found it amusing that women seemed to like the faintly misshapen nose. The same babe who'd said his eyes were like the sea had told him it made him look dangerous.

"Whatever turns you on," Jake had said with a husky laugh, as he rolled her beneath him.

And he had money. Hell, why dance around the issue? He was rich, richer than he'd ever dreamed he could be, and he'd earned every dime himself, transforming a propensity for numbers, a talent for reading the market and a love for taking risks into a career in venture capitalism that was light-years away from the life he'd been born to.

Wasn't all that enough to make a woman happy? Yes. Yes, it was. He never had difficulty finding a woman.

The trouble was getting rid of them.

Jake winced.

It wasn't a nice way to think about it but it was the truth.

What he was going through with Brandi wasn't exactly new. It had happened to him before. A woman would agree, at the start of their affair, that she was no more interested in forever-after than he was. Then, for some unearthly reason, she'd change her mind a few weeks later and get that oh-how-happy-we-could-be gleam in her eye even though any fool could tell that marriage was not man's natural state.

The whole turnaround was beyond his comprehension but yeah, it happened. And it was happening again, despite his best efforts.

The only person who could save him from disaster was his personal assistant, Emily.

Emily, Jake thought gratefully. What would he do without her? She was smart, efficient, always on her toes. Emily not only kept his office running smoothly, but she protected him from the predations of women like Brandi. It didn't happen often, thankfully, but when necessary, Emily fielded unwanted calls, kept away unwanted visitors.

Jake wasn't unkind. That was the reason he'd told Emily to show Brandi into his private office yesterday, even though he knew it was a bad idea. He was right. It had been a miserable idea. All Brandi had wanted to do was tell him that she loved him but he didn't love her.

"You don't," she'd cried, "you don't, Jake!"

Why would he deny it? "No," he'd said, "I don't." He'd

handed her his handkerchief. "But I like you," he'd added earnestly. "A lot."

Jake sighed, sat down at his desk, leaned his elbows on the gleaming oak surface and massaged his aching temples with his fingertips.

So much for being honest. Brandi had gone from weeping to sobbing while he stood there, feeling like an idiot for not having seen it coming but then, he really never did.

"Hell," he muttered, and shot to his feet again.

He really did like her. Why else would he have spent the last, what, two months seeing her? Exclusively, of course. He wasn't into sharing his women and besides, he was always faithful for as long as a relationship lasted. But he wasn't ready to spend the rest of his life with one woman. Not now, not in the foreseeable future, maybe not ever.

Life had only just begun to open for him in the past few years. Jake had grown up poor, lost his father in a mining accident when he was ten, lost his mother to a stepfather who believed that sparing the rod spoiled the child when he was twelve. At seventeen, he'd quit school and gone to work in the same mine that had taken his father's life. A year later, after almost dying under two tons of coal, Jake put down his hammer and scrubbed the black dust from his skin even though he'd known he'd never quite get it out of his blood. Then he'd headed east. It had taken a while but a quirky combination of luck, guts and a hard-won university degree had turned his life into a dream.

It was a life he liked, just the way it was.

He had an office in Rockefeller Center, an apartment on Park Avenue, a weekend house in Connecticut and a vintage Corvette.

He had Emily.

Yes, life was good…except for this current mess, with Brandi.

Jake groaned, kicked back his chair and put his feet up on his desk. How come he hadn't read the signs? Her career was all that mattered, she'd told him, but it wasn't true. First she gave him a key to her apartment. He hadn't asked for one, hadn't offered her the key to his, but she handed hers over, anyway, with a casual smile that would have made him look like an ass not to have accepted it. Then she bought him a tie at Bloomingdale's. Nobody bought Jake ties except Jake, but she said some hotshot actor had been wearing one just like it when she'd posed in an ad with him, and how could he possibly turn down such a simple gift?

And then, last week, the final touch. He'd taken her home, was in the process of saying good-night—he hadn't felt like spending the night with her which, in retrospect, he should have recognized as the beginning of the end—when she reached into her pocket, pulled out a pair of airline tickets and waggled them at him.

"Surprise," she'd said gaily, and explained that she was flying home to Minneapolis for the weekend and he was go-ing with her.

"It's my parents' thirty-fifth anniversary, Jake. They're having the whole family to dinner and they're just dying to meet you!"

The tie around his neck—the very one she'd bought him, which he hated but had worn that evening because she'd asked him where it was—suddenly felt like a noose, growing tighter and tighter until he stabbed two fingers under the knot and yanked it away from his throat.

"I can't go," he'd said, and she'd said yes, yes, he could, and he'd said he couldn't and she, with her lip trembling, said he could if he wanted to and finally he'd said well, he *didn't* want to...

"Oh, Jake," she'd whispered, and the next thing he'd known, she was crying into his shirt.

What did women want, anyway? Well, not all women. Not the Emilies of this world but then, Emily wasn't a woman. Not a real one. She was his P.A.

Jake sighed, rose from the chair behind his desk, walked

to the window and looked out. Forty stories below, people crowded the street. He hoped Brandi wasn't one of those people. She'd been there this morning, waiting for him.

"Jake?" she'd said, and before he could decide what the heck to do, whether to pretend he didn't see her or hustle her into the lobby and up to his office before she started bawling, she'd thrown her arms around him and tried to kiss him.

"Hell," he whispered, and leaned his forehead against the cool glass.

Still, he had no desire to hurt her. He didn't want to say anything cruel or unkind...

"Mr. McBride?"

Because she was a nice woman. And even though it was time to move on, that didn't mean—

"Mr. McBride? Sir?"

Jake swung around. Emily stood in the doorway. For the first time in what felt like hours, he smiled. If only all women were as pragmatic, as sensible, as she.

"Yes, Emily?"

"Sir, I thought you'd like to know that I sent that e-mail memo to John Woods."

"Fine."

"His reply just came in. He says he likes your suggestions and hopes you're free to fly to San Diego to meet with him next week."

"Am I?"

"Yes, sir. You're free Monday and Tuesday. You have a meeting Tuesday afternoon but it can be easily postponed."

Jake nodded. "Make the arrangements, please. What else?"

"A fax from Atlanta. Nothing important, just a confirmation of your conference call."

"Good, good. Anything else?"

Emily looked down at the notepad in her hand. "You're

having a late lunch with Mr. Carstairs tomorrow at the Oak Room.''

"Ah. Thank you for reminding me.''

"Yes, sir. And you have a dinner appointment this evening. Eight o'clock, at The Palm. You asked me to remind you to mention that new oil field opportunity in Russia.''

Jake smiled and shook his head. "What would I do without you?'' he said pleasantly. "You're the epitome of efficiency.''

"Being efficient is my job, Mr. McBride.''

"Jake, please. I don't think we need to be so formal. You've been working for me for, what, a year?''

"Eleven months and twelve days." Emily smiled politely. "I'm comfortable calling you Mr. McBride, sir. Unless *you* find it uncomfortable...?''

"No," Jake said quickly, "no, that's fine. Whatever you prefer is okay with me.''

It sure as hell was. He'd never had an assistant like this one. When he looked ahead, he could see Emily Taylor by his side well into the distant future. Emily wouldn't find a man, get married and quit her job. Her career meant as much to her as his did to him.

He was fairly certain she never even dated.

He supposed he ought to feel guilty for being happy she didn't, but why should he? Emily was just one of those women who wasn't interested in men. There was a long and honorable list of them, going back through the centuries. Betty Friedan and the women's libbers. The Suffragettes. Joan of Arc. They'd all devoted their lives to Causes, not to men.

How could a man feel badly if a woman made a choice like that?

Emily wasn't even a distraction.

Some of the women he'd interviewed before hiring her had been stunners, but the word for Emily was "average.''

Average height. Average weight. Average face. Average brown hair and average brown eyes.

"A little brown sparrow," Brandi had said after meeting her, with what Jake had recognized as a little purr of relief.

An accurate description, he thought. On his runs through Central Park, he saw lots of birds with flashier plumage but it was the little brown sparrows who were the most industrious.

Emily, Jake thought fondly. His very own little brown sparrow.

He smiled again, folded his arms and hitched a hip onto the edge of his desk. "Emily, how much am I paying you?"

"Sir?"

"Your salary. What is it?"

"Eight hundred a week, Mr. McBride."

"Well, give yourself a hundred bucks more."

Emily smiled politely. "Thank you, sir."

Jake smiled, too. He liked the no-nonsense way she'd accepted her raise. No little squeals of joy, no bouncing up and down, no "Oooh, Jake…" But, of course, she wouldn't call him "Jake" any more than she'd squeal. Squealing was for the women he dated, who greeted each bouquet of long-stemmed roses, each blue-boxed Tiffany trinket, with shrieks of delight.

"No." Jake strolled towards her. "No, thank *you*, Emily."

He clapped her lightly on the back. That was another thing he liked about his P.A. Her posture. She stood ramrod straight, not slouched or with her hips angled forward. So many women in New York stood that way, as if they were about to stalk down a runway at a fashion show.

Not his Emily.

Idly, he wondered what effect Emily's perfect stance had on her figure. Did it tilt her breasts forward? He couldn't tell; summer and winter, she always wore suits. Tweed, for the most part, like this one. Brown tweed, to match her brown hair, with the jacket closed so that her figure was pretty much a mystery. For all he knew, her breasts were the size of Ping-Pong balls. Or casaba melons. Who knew? Who cared? Not him. Yes, it was a definite pleasure to work with a woman who was both efficient and unattractive.

"I mean it," he said. "You're the best P.A. I've ever had."

Emily cleared her throat. "In that case, sir..."

"Yes?" Jake grinned. Evidently, the raise he'd just given her wasn't enough. That surprised him a little; Emily was never pushy but if she thought she deserved more money, she could have it. "Give yourself two hundred more a week. Is that better?"

A light blush suffused her cheeks. "One hundred is fine, Mr. McBride." She stepped back, her chin lifted, her eyes on his. "But I would much prefer to be called your E.A. instead of your P.A."

"Huh?"

"Your executive assistant, instead of your personal assistant. It's a more accurate description of my duties."

"My exec," Jake mused. "Well, sure. You want to be called my E.A., that's fine."

"Thank you again, sir."

"You're welcome." Jake smiled. "Just as long as you assure me you aren't changing your title to make your résumé look better."

"Sir?"

"You're not thinking of going job-hunting, are you?"

Emily looked horrified. "Certainly not, sir. I merely want an appropriate title."

Well, well, well. His little sparrow had an ego. Nothing wrong with that. Nothing at all.

"And you deserve it."

Oh, the sickly-sweet benevolence in his tone. Emily smiled, not an easy thing to do when what she felt like doing was throwing up on Jake McBride's shiny black shoes. The egotistical goon. If only she could tell him what she thought of him. But she couldn't. Jobs as good as this one were impossible to find. She had lots of responsibility; the pay was excellent; and, she supposed, as men went, McBride was easy enough to work for. She just wondered if he had any idea, any actual idea, of how invaluable she was to him. Of what a mess he'd be in, without her.

Why wonder? She knew that he didn't. He was as dense as every other man she'd ever known, as foolishly arrogant as the endless succession of idiots who'd trooped through the house when she was growing up, every last one of them thinking he knew what he was doing and why he was doing it when, in reality, her gorgeous sisters had been leading the jerks around by their...hormones.

Jake McBride was just like those silly stud puppies. He might be rich, he might be handsome—assuming you liked the type, which she certainly didn't—but he was as much a victim of his hormones as the tongue-tied idiots who'd filled her sisters' teenaged lives.

His problems with the latest twit was proof of that.

McBride had broken things off. No surprise there. Emily had sensed it coming, long before he had. And, she had to admit, he'd done it with his usual flair. Roses. A little bracelet from Tiffany's that she knew—after all, she'd placed the order—set him back six thousand dollars. But the brunette with the ditzy name wouldn't, couldn't, accept The End. She sent gifts. Notes. She phoned. She'd even taken to dropping by the office.

I'm here to see Jake, she'd whisper, in a voice Marilyn Monroe would have envied.

And Emily would pick up the phone, tell her boss that Miss Carole was here. And McBride would say, oh Lord, just get rid of her, please, Emily.

Emily almost felt sorry for the woman. She certainly didn't feel sorry for Jake. As if she had nothing better to do than clean up after his messes. Bad enough she'd cleaned up after messes that involved her sisters.

Em, are you sure Billy hasn't called? Or, *Em, I'm so unhappy. Jimmy's dating another girl.* And then, after they both got married, she'd been expected to soothe them through their other disasters. *Em, I think Billy's fooling around. Em, Jimmy just doesn't love me the way he used to...*

They hadn't learned anything, either, not even after marriages and divorces and affairs...

Ridiculous, the way women set out to snare men and ended up in the trap, themselves.

That had never been what she wanted out of life. A man? A lot of embarrassing slobbering to be endured and then, maybe, a wedding ring and promises of forever-after that wouldn't even last as long as it took a slice of good-luck wedding cake to go stale, and for what?

For companionship, Emily. For those long winter nights when you think you'll die if you have to curl up with another book...

Emily bit her lip.

Okay. So, maybe she wasn't getting any younger. Maybe it might be nice to know what it was like to go on an occasional date. To have some man send her flowers, the way McBride—correction. The way *she* sent flowers, to his women. It might even be nice to get to see all those elegant New York restaurants from the inside, instead of just telephoning to make reservations for her boss and his latest interest.

What would such an evening be like? To have a man smile across the table at you, have him pick up your hand and bring it to his lips? Even if she really wanted to find out, where would she find a date? Lately, she'd started reading through the Personals in the back of *GOTHAM* magazine. Just for laughs, of course. She couldn't imagine ever bringing herself to answer an ad. Or running one. What would she say?

Average-looking mouse searching for gorgeous, sexy, exciting man but will settle for plain, nonsexy, unexciting, average-looking rat...

No. That wouldn't do at all. Then again, neither would the truth.

Average-looking female interested in average-looking male. Object: to find out what a date is like because said female hasn't had one in forever. In fact, not since the night of her senior prom, when one of her beautiful sisters conned a would-be boyfriend into being said female's date and everybody knew it and laughed...

"Emily?"

Okay. That was it. She *would* run an ad. After all, she wasn't eighteen anymore. She wasn't Serena and Angela Taylor's poor little sister, the one with all the brains and none of the looks. She wasn't one of Jake McBride's women, either, with the kind of face and figure men dreamed of, but she could still manage to find herself a date—

"Emily? Are you okay?"

A large, warm hand settled on her shoulder. Emily blinked, focused her eyes on her boss. He was standing a breath away from her, staring at her with a little furrow just between his eyes. And what eyes they were. Dark. Deep. So deep...

"Are you all right? For a minute there, you seemed to drift away."

"I'm fine," she said briskly. "Just, uh, just a cold coming on, perhaps."

His hand slid to her elbow. "Go home," he said gently, as he propelled her towards the door. "Take a nice hot bath. Make yourself some tea."

"Honestly, Mr. McBride..."

"Do it," he said, with a polite, teasing smile, "or I'll take you home and do it for you."

An image swam into her head. McBride, in her tiny apartment, so big and masculine against her chintz-covered furniture. McBride, smiling down at her, his hands warm and gentle as he unbuttoned her tweed jacket, unbuttoned her silk blouse. Or, perhaps, his hands not so gentle. Hard, in fact.

Rough, maybe, as he ripped the blouse from her and took her into his arms…

Color flooded her face as she stepped back.

"That won't be necessary, sir. I'm perfectly capable of taking care of myself."

"I know you are," he said. For one awful minute, she was afraid he was going to pat her on the head. "Now just run along home, Emily. Take that bath, have the tea, pop some vitamin C and get a good night's rest."

"But it's only four forty-five."

McBride gave her another of those I'm-So-Wonderful-and-You're-So-Lucky-To-Be-Working-For-Me smiles.

"I can do without you for a little while, I promise. Now, go home. I'll see you in the morning."

"Thank you, Mr. McBride."

"Good night, Emily."

"Good night, sir."

Jake shut the door and sat down at his desk. Damn, what dedication. He'd almost had to carry Emily out of the office. Well, that would have been simple enough. She was small. Slender. She'd be light, just like one of those little sparrows. He could carry Emily up the steps in his duplex, to his bedroom, set her down on her feet and find out just what, exactly, lay hidden under all those woolly layers of clothing…

He frowned, pulled a blank pad towards him. What crazy thoughts. Jake chuckled softly. Amazing, the things a man's brain could conjure up at the end of a long day. Better to spend the next couple of hours profitably, writing some memos to leave on Emily's desk for her to tackle first thing in the morning.

He worked for a while, went from the memos to sketching out an idea that had just come to him about that meeting in San Diego…

A knock sounded on the door.

Jake looked up, then checked his watch. It was after five. Emily was gone. Nobody else would…

Somebody would.

Brandi, he thought unhappily. She'd called earlier, when Emily was at lunch. He'd picked up the phone just as the answering machine did and he'd heard that little whisper that had once driven him crazy with lust and now just drove him crazy, begging him to see her tonight.

The knock came again. Maybe if he just sat it out, pretended he wasn't here...

"Jake?"

The door swung open. Jake, caught between deciding whether to duck for cover or tell Brandi to get lost, looked up and grinned in surprise.

"Pete?"

Pete Archer, a guy he'd worked with his first year in New York, opened the door wider and stepped inside.

"Jake, you old son of a gun. What's the matter? You afraid I'm a bill collector or something?"

Jake got to his feet. "Or something." He came forward and the men shook hands. They'd never been close friends but it was great to see someone from the past. "Why didn't you call me? If I'd known you were going to be in town, I'd have rolled out the red carpet."

"Didn't know it, until the last minute." Pete smiled. "You look like life's treating you well."

"You, too." Jake grinned, gave Pete a light jab to the biceps. "How long will you be in town?"

"Just overnight. I have to be back in Chicago tomorrow morning."

"Too bad. I have a business dinner lined up. Let me call the guy and—"

"No, no, I understand. How about drinks? You have time for that?"

"Great idea. Want to go out, or have something here?"

"Here would be cool. Got any ale?"

Jake laughed. "Some things never change, huh? Ale, it is."

He went to his built-in mini fridge, took out a couple of bottles and opened them. Pete wáved away his offer of a glass. The two men sat across from each other, leaned close enough to clink bottles, took long, thirsty swallows, then smiled.

"So," Jake said, "how're things?"

"Couldn't be better. And you?"

"Terrific." Jake sighed. "Well, they would be, if…" He leaned forward, across the desk. "You know why I didn't answer when you knocked? I thought you were a woman."

Pete laughed. "Don't tell me you've decided you're giving up babes. I wouldn't believe it."

"Let me amend that," Jake said, smiling. "I thought you were a particular woman."

"Ah. A bowwow who's developed a thing for you, huh?"

"No, she's a definite ten." Jake grinned, but his grin faded. "But the thing ran its course, you know? She began to hear wedding bells."

"Oh, yeah. I know what that's like." Pete drank some ale. "So, you tried to end it?"

"I'm still trying. Trouble is, she's determined. She calls. She sends me notes. She shows up at my apartment, she shows up here…"

"Well, you have a secretary, don't you? Let her do the dirty work."

"I have an executive assistant," Jake said, smiling and lifting his eyebrows.

"What's that mean?"

"It means I'm lucky enough to employ a woman whose only goal in life is to make me happy."

"Jake, you dog, you! You stocked the front desk with a hot babe!"

"Sorry to burst the bubble, pal, but Emily's as far from being a hot babe as Arnold Schwarzenegger."

Pete sighed. "Too bad. I figured her for the fox I just saw at the elevator."

"Oh, hell," Jake said, and the color drained from his face. "Brunette?"

"Uh-huh."

"Big brown eyes?"

"Uh-huh."

"Great legs? A body meant to send a man straight over the edge?"

Pete shrugged, took a drink of his ale. "Definitely and probably."

"Probably?" Jake gave a forlorn laugh. "You'd have to be blind or dead not to notice Brandi's figure."

"Brandi?"

"Yeah. The lady who's decided I'm the love of her life. I half-figured she might show up here tonight."

"Well, she did. And the only reason I didn't notice her shape was because it was hidden under a layer of tweed."

"Yeah, well…" Jake stared at Pete. "Tweed? Brandi would sooner be caught during rush hour in a New York subway than in tweed."

"Either her tastes have changed, or the woman I saw wasn't… Who'd you say?"

"Brandi," Jake said automatically. He frowned. "Emily wears tweed."

"And Emily would be…?"

"I told you about her. She's my P.A. My E.A." Jake thought for a second, then shook his head. "Forget it. No way could it have been Emily. I mean, she's great. She's efficient. She's capable. She's the best assistant I've ever had." He smiled. "But a looker? No way."

Pete gave a dramatic sigh. "See, that's where we differ, Jake. I've learned to refine my tastes."

Jake grinned. "Sure."

"No, I'm serious. I look beyond the obvious." He leaned forward, gave a leering smirk. "Besides, you know what they say. Still waters run deep."

"Meaning?"

"Meaning," Pete said smugly, "if a babe doesn't think she's a looker, a guy can get into her pants a lot easier."

Jake shot to his feet. "Not into Emily's, he can't." His voice was cold; he could feel the sudden tension in his muscles.

"Hey." Pete stood up, too. "We don't even know it's Emily we're talking about."

"I'm just making a point, Archer. Forget about getting into Emily's pants."

"Yeah, but it's probably not even... Jake. I didn't..." Pete took a breath. "Listen man, no offence."

"None taken," Jake said, and even he could hear the lie in his words. Well, why wouldn't he be upset? Emily was a fantastic asset. He wasn't about to end up with a messed-up assistant on his hands. Anyway, it was all academic, he thought, and forced himself to smile. "Not that it matters. That couldn't have been Emily. She isn't a looker. You don't know my Emily but I can tell you, my Emily is average—"

"Your Emily isn't 'your Emily,' Mr. McBride!"

Both men swung around. Emily stood in the open doorway, her face pale except for two spots of crimson high on her cheeks.

"Oh, hell," Jake said softly. "Emily. Emily, listen, I didn't mean—"

"You *did* mean. And I don't mind being called 'average.' It's what I am." Her hands bunched into fists, fists she hid in the folds of her tweed skirt. "But I am not your property. You may assume I have no life away from this office, but that does not give you the right to—"

"Emily," Jake said unhappily, "please—"

"Emily." Pete's voice was soft. Smarmy, Jake thought. Gentle, Emily thought, and looked at him. "Emily," Pete said again, and smiled, "I'm sorry we have to meet under such difficult circumstances."

"You two were talking about me," she said stiffly.

Pete walked towards her. "We were, yes. I was telling Jake—Mr. McBride—that I'd just passed you in the hall."

Jake made a choked sound. "You mean, the woman you were talking about really was—"

"And that I wanted to meet you," Pete went on, as if Jake hadn't spoken. He held out his hand. "My name is Pete Archer."

Emily ignored his outstretched hand. "Why did you want to meet me?"

"Because I'd like to take you to dinner."

"Nonsense." Jake's voice was too loud, too sharp. He knew it but hell, this was his office and his exec. What right did Archer have to... "She can't go with you," he said, as he stalked towards the two of them. "She doesn't want to go with you. She—"

"I'd be delighted," Emily said firmly.

"Emily, don't be a fool. Pete's not really interested in..." Jake bit his lip. If looks could kill, the one she'd just given him would have left him stone-cold and on the way to the mortuary. "For heaven's sake, where's your common sense? You, and this man...?"

She shot him a look more vicious than the first, and then she swung towards Pete.

"Shall we go, Mr. Archer?"

"Archer," Jake roared, "you son of a—"

"The lady's made her decision, Jake."

"I have, indeed. You pay my salary, Mr. McBride, but you do not own me. I do as I wish after office hours. If I want to go out on a date, I will." Her eyes narrowed. "Unless you'd rather I tendered my resignation...?"

Emily waited. Pete did, too. And Jake, totally helpless for the first time in his adult life, could do nothing except stand in the center of his office and watch his former friend and his little brown sparrow flutter her wings as she headed for a night on the town.

CHAPTER TWO

THE city awoke to snow the next morning.

Heavy wet flakes drifted down from the skies.

Fine, Jake thought. Let the sky turn to lead, for all he cared. He was in a mood almost as foul as the weather. Snow that would soon turn to gray slush was just about right this morning.

The doorman greeted him cheerfully. Jake muttered a response, waved off his offer of a taxi. Traffic in Manhattan always verged on gridlock; it would be even worse in weather like this. Besides, walking to work might be a good idea. He figured that the cold air, a brisk pace as he headed crosstown, would improve his mood.

It didn't.

Some bozo trying to get his truck through a blocked intersection sent a spray of wet, dirty snow flying onto the sidewalk and over Jake's shoes; a guy on Rollerblades—Rollerblades, on a day like this—damned near rode him down.

By the time he reached Rockefeller Center, Jake's mood had gone from glum to grim. He gave a cursory look around as he strode into the building but he knew Brandi would be a no-show on a day like this. Not even her sudden determination to keep their affair alive would stand up to the possibility that her hair or makeup might get damaged. It was an unkind thought but, dammit, he was in an unkind frame of mind.

That was what staying awake half the night did to a man. Left him ill-tempered and mean-natured, especially when there was no good reason for him to have spent more time pacing the floors than sleeping.

It had to be the caffeine, Jake thought, as he stepped from

the elevator onto the pale gray marble floor and walked to his office. The health food pundits made him edgy, with all their doomsaying. He liked coffee, and steak, and if he'd ever accidentally consumed a bite of tofu in his life, he didn't want to know it.

Still, what else could have kept him up until almost dawn, if it wasn't caffeine? Or maybe that Chinese takeout he'd picked up for supper had done him in. Not that he'd eaten much of it. Jake frowned as he reached his office. A hell of a night he'd put in, not eating, not sleeping...

The kid who delivered the mail came skidding around the corner.

"Morning, Mr. McBride," he said cheerfully. "Here's your mail."

Jake, in no mood for cheerful banter or a stack of mail, scowled at the kid.

"What's the matter?" he growled. "Don't you deliver it anymore?"

"I am delivering it. See?" The kid shoved an armload of stuff at Jake, who took it grudgingly.

"This goes to my P.A., not to me."

"Your what?"

"My P.A. My E.A...." Jake's scowl deepened. "My secretary," he said. "You're supposed to hand her the mail."

"Oh. Emily."

For reasons unknown, Jake felt his hackles rise. "Her name," he said coldly, "is Miss Taylor."

"Uh-huh. Emily, like I said." The kid grinned. "Nice lady. Pretty eyes."

What was this? Did every male who walked in the door have to make an appraisal of Emily? What about her eyes? She had two of them. So what? Most people did.

"I always hand the mail right to her. But the door's locked. It looks like nobody's home."

Jake's scowl turned to a look of disbelief. He shot back

the cuffs of his Burberry and his suit jacket, checked his watch and looked at the kid.

"Don't be ridiculous. Of course someone is home." He grabbed the doorknob. "It's after nine. Miss Taylor's always at her desk by—"

The knob didn't move. The kid was right. The door was locked.

Jake's mood, already in the cellar, began digging its way towards China. He shifted the armload of envelopes and magazines, dug out his keys and let himself into his office.

"If Emily is sick or something," the kid said, "when you talk to her, tell her that Tommy sends—"

Jake slammed the door, stalked across the office and dumped the mail on Emily's desk. It was, as always, neat as a pin. Even when she was seated behind it, not so much as a paper clip was ever out of place. Still, he could tell she wasn't there. Her computer monitor stared at him with a cold black eye. The office lights were off, too, and there was no wonderful aroma of fresh coffee in the air.

E.A. or not, Emily had no feminist compunction against making coffee every morning.

Jake turned on the lights, marched into his private office, peeled off his wet coat and dumped it on the back of his chair.

Sick? Emily?

"Ha," he said.

She hadn't been sick a day since she'd come to work for him. Yeah, she'd said she felt as if she were coming down with a cold yesterday afternoon but it couldn't have been much of a cold because not an hour later, she'd leaped at Archer's invitation to dinner like a trout going after a fly.

"Sick," Jake muttered.

Sleeping off her big night out, was more like it. Who knew where Archer had taken her for dinner, or what hour he'd gotten her home? Who knew how much wine she'd had to drink or how late she'd gone to bed or if she'd gone to bed at all...

Or if she'd been alone when she got into it.

Not that he cared. What she did, who she did it with, was her business. He'd tell her that, when—if—she deigned to show up this morning. The only question was, should he tell it to her before or after he told her she was fired?

From executive assistant to unemployed, in less than twenty-four hours.

The thought did wonders for his disposition. But why wait for Miss Taylor to put in an appearance? He could just as easily fire her right now.

Jake smiled coldly as he reached for the telephone but his smile changed, went back to being a frown. What was her number? For that matter, where did she live? In the city? In the suburbs? In one of the outlying boroughs? He had all that information. She'd filled out a form when she'd come to work for him. Actually, she'd filled out a zillion forms, thanks to all the tax information everybody required, but he'd be damned if he could remember anything about Emily's private life.

Why would he? Until Archer stirred things up, she'd been the perfect employee. He'd never had reason to think about her, once he was away from the office. And now he was wasting time, thinking about her instead of sitting down and doing all the things that needed doing today. Not that he was actually "thinking" about Emily. Where she'd gone with Archer. Whether she'd had fun. Whether Archer had come on to her. Whether she was late because, even now, she was lying in the bastard's arms...

"Son of a bitch," Jake said, under his breath.

He thumbed open his address book, ran his finger down the list of T's. There it was, Emily Taylor, the phone number written in Emily's own, careful hand. Her address was there, too. She lived in Manhattan. Good, he thought grimly as he punched the phone number into the keypad. Then, she could damned well get her tail in here, pronto, and never mind what she was in the middle of doing with Archer.

Let her trudge through the snow. Then, he'd fire her. In person, where he could watch her face become pale as he told her to get out of his life.

Jake waited, tapping his foot impatiently as the phone rang. And rang. And—

"Good morning, Mr. McBride."

"I'm happy you think so, Miss Taylor," he said coldly...and suddenly realized that Emily's voice wasn't coming from the phone in his hand, it was coming from behind him. Slowly, he put down the telephone and turned around.

She stood in the doorway. Snowflakes glittered in her hair—brown hair, he thought, but with a warm, golden glow that made a man think of dark maple syrup on a winter morning....

Jake's mouth turned down.

"You're late."

"I'm aware of that, sir. And I'm sorry."

She didn't sound sorry. Not the least bit. There was a chill to her voice that had nothing to do with the weather.

"And you're late because...?"

"The trains are running behind schedule."

"Really." Jake smiled thinly and folded his arms. "I wonder if that could be because it's snowing."

He was gratified to see a light flush color her cheeks. "I'm sure it is, Mr. McBride."

"In which case, Miss Taylor, you must also know that the trains always run late when it snows. Half the city runs late—or is that news to you?"

Emily looked down and brushed the snow from her coat. Her ankle-length, tweed coat, Jake thought irritably. Was tweed the only item in her wardrobe? Was he ever going to see her legs?

"I know what snow does to New York," she said calmly. She lifted her eyes to his. "I allowed for that contingency."

"Ah. You allowed for it." Jake glanced pointedly at his watch. "Interesting, since you're almost an hour late."

Damn, he sounded like an ass. Well, so what? He was the boss. He was entitled to sound like an ass, if he wanted.

"I'm twenty minutes late, sir." Emily still sounded calm but there was a bite to the "sir." "And I did allow for the weather. I left my apartment twenty minutes earlier than usual. If I hadn't, I'd be later than I already am."

"Does that mean you got out of bed twenty minutes earlier than usual?"

Emily's eyebrows brows rose. "I beg your pardon?"

"It's a simple question. I asked if you set your alarm back twenty minutes."

"I don't see what that has to do with anything."

Neither did Jake. What he really wanted to ask was if she'd had to set the alarm back or if something else had awakened her this morning. Somebody. Archer, for instance, moving above her, in her bed...

Hell!

Jake frowned, cleared his throat, went behind his desk and sat down. He reached for his appointment book and looked at the page. Letters and numbers danced before his eyes.

"Never mind," he said brusquely.

"Never mind, indeed." Her voice was frigid now; he could almost see the icicles forming on each word. "Perhaps we need to establish some boundaries, Mr. McBride. My private life—"

"So you said, last evening." Jake waved his hand in dismissal. "I left the mail on your desk. Go through it, see if anything needs my immediate attention and then come back and I'll dictate some notes."

She hesitated. He didn't look up but he didn't have to. He could all but feel her counting to ten, taking deep breaths, doing what she could to hang onto her composure. Well, wasn't he doing the same thing? The nerve of her, holding him up for a pay raise and a new title one day and coming in late the next.

"Of course, Mr. McBride."

The door snicked shut. Jake looked up, glowered at it, and closed his appointment book.

Of course, Mr. McBride, he thought furiously. As if nothing had changed, as if she hadn't shown up late, been insubordinate, done exactly the opposite of what he'd told her to do and gone off with a man who was only after one thing…

Jake closed his eyes. "Hell," he said, but with no heat whatsoever.

Emily was right. Her life, outside of the office, wasn't his business. Who she dated was up to her. What she did with who she dated was up to her, too. Why should he care, as long as she did her work?

Still, it was only human to wonder where she'd gone last night and whether she'd had a good time. He could just ask her. He'd known Emily for almost a year now. They were friends. Well, they were business associates. And he'd been the one who'd put Archer in her path.

Was it so strange he should be vaguely curious about how things had gone last night?

Emily, he could say, *I was just wondering, did you have a nice evening? Where'd Archer take you for dinner? Did he take you home? Did you invite him in? What time did he leave?*

He did leave, didn't he?

Jake rubbed his hands over his face.

Not only was her private life none of his business, but even thinking about it was none of his business.

The kid was right, though. She did have nice eyes.

A muscle knotted in Jake's jaw. He wondered if Archer had been right, too. About her legs. Were they great? He couldn't tell, not with that coat going straight down to her feet, and he'd certainly never noticed her legs in the past.

Why would he? Emily was his P.A. Check that. She was his E.A. She was a well-oiled, well-educated, well-paid employee. Her looks were none of his business.

She was a quiet little sparrow.

His little sparrow.

Jake shoved the appointment book halfway across his desk, swiveled his chair towards the window and gave the falling snow the benefit of his scowl. He knew it was foolish to bristle, but bristling was precisely what he felt like doing.

And it was all Emily's fault.

Emily took off her coat, shook it briskly and hung it in the closet. Then she sat, bent down and began tugging at her left boot while she told herself that bristling would get her nowhere.

Still, bristling was exactly what she felt like doing.

And it was all McBride's fault.

The great man was not in a good mood this morning. Too bad. Perhaps he'd had another run-in with the twit, desperate to tell him how wonderful he was.

"Idiot," Emily said, and gave the stubborn boot a whack.

Or was he still annoyed that she hadn't let him tell her what to do last night? Don't go, he'd said, as if he owned her, and the hell of it was she should have listened to him because her evening with his pal had been a disaster. A total, unmitigated disaster. Mr. Peter-Aren't-You-Fortunate-To-Be-With-Me Archer was so full of himself it was a wonder there'd been room for her at their all-too-cozy table for two in the restaurant he'd chosen.

Emily hung her head and groaned.

Oh, what an awful evening. The wine he'd ordered, even after she'd politely declined a drink. The way he'd leaned close and breathed moistly on her neck. The way he'd tried to feed her a bite of his meal from his fork. Yuck. As if she would want to take the fork into her mouth after it had been in his. And then all that smarmy, double entendre stuff which she'd been too dumb to recognize as smarmy and double entendre, until the waiter happened by just as Archer, the slimeball, said something that made the hapless waiter almost pour the coffee into her lap.

Emily attacked the boot again.

And this man, she reminded herself grimly, this—this human octopus, was Mr. Jake McBride's friend. His oldest, dearest, closest friend.

So much for thinking her boss was a nice guy even if he was dense. Nice guys didn't have lifelong buddies like Peter Archer.

Damn this boot! Why wouldn't it come off?

To think of McBride's gall, that *he* was angry with *her*. Whatever the cause of it, how dare he take it out on her? She'd been, what, fifteen minutes late? When she thought of all the times she'd come in early without McBride so much as saying, Why, Emily, how good of you to be here before nine.

But why would he? She was his personal property. He expected her to be there, at his beck and call.

"The Emperor McBride," she said, under her breath, and tugged harder. What was with these boots? They might as well be glued on.

"Uh," she said, and tugged again. "Uh..."

"Having a problem, Emily?"

She sat up so fast that her heel slammed against the carpeted floor. McBride was standing in the doorway, watching her. His arms were folded and one of his dark eyebrows was lifted in what looked like amusement.

"No problem, sir," she replied briskly.

Of course it was a problem. She'd been bent over, tugging at her boots, and her face was flushed with rosy color. Her hair—a few strands of it, anyway—had come loose of its clip at the nape of her neck and curled gently at her ears. Emily's hair was curly? He'd never noticed. She always wore it back, and straight.

Jake frowned.

"Here," he said, advancing towards her, "let me help you."

"It isn't necessary. I can—"

Too late. He was already squatting before her, lifting her foot into his lap and tugging.

"Really, Mr. McBride…"

Jake pulled off the boot. No wonder it had been hard to remove. Her boots were made of thin black leather and she was wearing heavy socks. Heavy wool socks, over feet that were attached to long, slender legs.

Oh, yeah. Archer, the bastard, had called it right. Her legs were good. Excellent, as a matter of fact.

"Thank you," Emily said.

Jake lifted his eyes to her face. "You're welcome." He cleared his throat, looked down at the foot, still in his hands, and tried to think of something intelligent to say. "You're wearing socks." Brilliant, he thought trying not to wince, just brilliant, McBride. "I mean—you're wearing—"

"Socks," she said stiffly. "Wool socks. Double knit. I guess that's the reason the boots are so hard to get off. I wore them because I thought I might have to walk at least part of the way home, if the snow keeps up, and these boots aren't really warm…"

Her voice trailed to silence. Why was she telling him all this? He was holding her foot in his hands, looking at it as if he'd never seen a foot before. And she was explaining why she was wearing wool socks, as if it mattered.

"Socks," he murmured, and looked up at her again. He had such a strange look on his face. That darkness in his eyes.

Maybe he thought she was going to walk around the office in heavy wool socks all day.

"Yes. But I'll take them off. I have panty hose underneath…"

Oh, good. Now she was telling him about her underwear. Emily colored and pulled her foot from Jake's hands.

"Thank you again," she said briskly. "I'll get to the mail immediately."

"Not without taking that other boot off."

"I can manage."

"I doubt it."

"Honestly, Mr. McBride—"

Jake knew he could get the boot off with one quick tug but considering the condition she'd put him in, with that comment about her underwear, he figured it was best to take his time.

"There," he said, when it was safe. He dropped the boot beside its mate and rose to his feet. "All done."

Emily nodded. "Thank you," she said again.

"You're welcome."

He looked as if he were going to say something more. A few words of apology, maybe, for the way he'd snapped at her before? No such luck. He gave her a quick nod, swung away and went back inside his office.

The door closed silently behind him.

Emily sat motionless. Her feet were tingling. Not the way they'd tingle if the circulation were coming back after they'd been freezing cold. She'd felt that, once, when she was a little girl and she'd missed the school bus and ended up walking home in the snow. No, they were tingling in a very strange way. As if they were still in McBride's lap. As if his big hands were still holding them. As if he were still looking up at her with his eyes all dark and hungry...

The room seemed to tilt.

Emily dragged air into her lungs. Then she took off her socks, slipped her feet into the shoes she'd brought with her, and got to work.

Hours later, she sighed, blinked owlishly at her computer screen and pushed back from her desk. It was almost one o'clock. Time for lunch, she thought, and rose from her chair. She gave a ladylike stretch, opened the drawer to get her purse...and saw the copy of *GOTHAM,* still opened to the personal ads.

She made a face, picked up the magazine and dumped it into the wastebasket.

"Goodbye and good riddance," she said, and dusted off her hands.

Last night had cured her of even thinking about going out for an evening with a man she didn't know anything about.

On the other hand, choosing a date from the Personals would be different.

She might not really "know" the man, but she wouldn't go into it blindfolded. At least, she'd have some information about her date beforehand. And she wouldn't have to waste an entire evening. She could suggest they meet for lunch, or coffee, or for nothing more complicated than a walk in the park. She could control the character of this kind of date and not end up finding out, as she had last night, that the only thing the man in question wanted was to get into her pants.

Emily plucked the discarded magazine from the wastebasket, opened it and laid it on her desk.

Handsome, sexy, successful male, 40, D, Br & Br, ISO beautiful, sexy female, preferably br&br, too...

Handsome, successful, sexy, Romeo, 33, S, BL and bl, looking for his beautiful, sexy Juliet...

Sexy, handsome guy, 38, ND, blond and blue, very successful, ISO sexy, beautiful lady, preferably Br&B...

It was like reading a code. ISO for "in search of." D for "divorced," S for "single," ND for "newly divorced." B's for hair and eye color. Unless you had red hair. Or gold. Or...

Oh, this was ridiculous. Advertisements by men for women. Reading them was a joke. They were so phony. If every guy who was dateless in New York was sexy, easy on the eyes and successful, why were they running these ads? She knew better than to fall for all those adjectives. In fact, if she had to come up with the name of a gorgeous, sexy, successful man, the only one she'd be able to muster was that of Jake Mc...

Emily's heartbeat stumbled. Quickly, she grabbed the telephone, punched in the Personals number, listened impatiently as a recorded female voice offered available options.

To reply to a LoveNote, the voice said nasally, *please enter the number of the LoveNote you've selected.*

Emily entered a number. She waited, heard a husky male voice say "hello," listened to what was, more or less, a repeat of the ad in the magazine, and waited for the ad to end and the tone to sound. At last, it did. It was time to leave a message for Mr. Handsome, Sexy and Successful, 40, D, brown and brown.

Her mouth was dry as sand. She thought, fleetingly, of the sad red geranium sitting at home on her kitchen table, which she kept forgetting to water...

Beeeep!

Emily swallowed, licked her lips and took a breath. Sound sexy, she told herself.

"Good afternoon." Great. Just great. She sounded about as sexy as a Girl Scout trying to sell cookies. "Hi," she said, trying for perky, if not sexy. "Uh, I'm calling to say—to say that I think I might be just the Brrr and Brrr—uh, the Brown and Brown you're looking for." She hesitated, checked the ad again. Sexy, it said. And beautiful. Emily chewed on her lip. "Well, maybe not. I mean, I have brown hair. And brown eyes. But I'm not exactly sexy. Or beautiful." Her voice cracked. "But, really, is that so awful? 'Beautiful' means having qualities that delight the senses. I know that because I had to look it up once, in the dictionary. I wanted the exact meaning because I was writing a term paper on Shelley. The poet, you know? Anyway, I'm just saying that beauty is in the eye of the beholder and handsome probably is, too. So even if you're not as handsome as you say you are, that's okay because I'm not..." She groaned, put her hand to her forehead. "As for sexy, well, what does 'sexy' mean, anyway? Different things in different cultures. For example, when I was studying anthro, I learned that sexual attractiveness varies enormously from tribe to tribe in the Amazon. Some view nudity as the norm. Others, perhaps after they've had some contact with the outside world, disdain nudity but see nothing wrong with indulging in coitus with a variety of partners. There's a particular pygmy tribe—"

A large male hand slammed down on the telephone cradle, breaking the connection. Emily jerked her head up. McBride was standing over her, looking down and glaring.

"Just what in the Sam Hill are you doing?"

Dear God, Emily thought, what *was* I doing? The telephone buzzed in her ear like an angry bee.

"Miss Taylor?"

"You've—you've always called me Emily."

"A mistake," Jake said coldly, "considering that I'm starting to realize I don't know the first thing about you."

He folded his arms over his chest. It was, she thought foolishly, a formidable chest. He'd taken off his suit jacket, loosened his tie, undone the top button of his white shirt and rolled back his sleeves. He did that often; he'd once said he felt choked in a suit and tie. Why was it she'd never before noticed that his arms were dusted with dark, silky-looking hair? That his chest was the width of The Great Wall of China?

"Well, Miss Taylor? What were you doing?"

Emily put the phone down, folded her hands in her lap and tried not to think about how long he might have been standing there.

"I was—I was making a call," she said carefully.

"To whom?"

"To…" She frowned as she looked up at him again. "It was a personal call, Mr. McBride."

"Yes." Jake shot her a predatory smile. "I imagined it was. Somehow or other, I didn't think you'd be discussing pygmy sex practices with any of my clients."

She could feel the heat flash into her face. "I was not discussing pygmy sex practices."

"What were you discussing, then?"

"Would you step back, please," she said coolly, "so I can stand up?"

"Answer the question, Miss Taylor."

"I don't have to." She could feel her courage rushing back, swirling through her blood in a wave of heat. "As I said, it was personal."

"Did you ask me if you could make personal calls?"

She blinked. "No. No, I didn't. But you never said—"

"You never asked."

Emily glowered up at Jake. "I'll pay for the call," she snapped.

"I don't want your money. I want to know why you were talking about pygmy sex practices, and with whom."

"Dammit!" She shoved her chair back and shot to her feet, her flushed, angry face lifted to Jake's. "I wasn't talking about pygmy sex practices. I told you that. I was leaving a message on an answering machine."

"An answering machine at the Museum of Natural History?"

God, that infuriating smirk on his face! How had she survived it, all this time?

"An answering machine at a man's apartment," she said tightly. Well, it wasn't a lie. It wasn't an apartment but Handsome, Sexy and Successful would probably phone in for his messages from his apartment.

"Well, well, well." Jake's dark green eyes narrowed.

"You're just full of surprises, Miss Taylor. No wonder ol'
Pete was so eager to take you to dinner last night. He read
you just right."

Emily flung her hands on her hips. "And what is that
supposed to mean, Mr. McBride?"

"Never mind what it's supposed to mean. I'm waiting to
hear who you were phoning."

"Oh, for goodness sake!" She swung away, grabbed the
magazine and shoved it into Jake's flat belly. "You won't
be satisfied until you wring the truth out of me, will you?
Okay. Okay, here's the truth, McBride, and I hope you enjoy
getting the last laugh."

She swung away from him, trembling with anger and humiliation. She could hear Jake reading the ads aloud in a soft,
disbelieving voice. There was a long silence before he spoke
again.

"You were answering an ad in the personals?"

"Yes."

"You were telling one of these men you'd go out with
him?"

"Yes."

"You were going to meet a stranger, an asshole who iden-
tifies himself as sexy, successful and handsome with... What
in hell is Brrr and Brrr? A description of the weather? A new
liqueur?"

Emily spun around and faced Jake. Her eyes were huge,
her face flushed, and he fought back the sudden, insane desire
to take her in his arms and soothe her.

"It's brown hair and brown eyes," she snarled. "And for
your information, lots of people meet through ads like this."

"To do what?" Jake said, his eyes getting that narrowed,
intense look again.

"To—to go out. On a date. To have dinner together. Take
in a movie. Just—just spend a little time with another person..."

Her voice broke. Jake looked bewildered. She thought, for a second, he was reaching towards her and she shook her head and stepped back.

"I don't expect you to understand. You're never home alone, unless you want to be. You never have to look at the calendar and say, look at that, it's the weekend and I don't have a thing to do except clean my apartment and wash my hair."

Holy hell, Jake thought.

"That's what this is all about?" he said slowly. "That you don't date?"

"That's what I just said."

"You don't have any, uh, any men in your life?"

Emily's chin lifted to a dangerous angle. "Are we going to have to go through this, line by line?"

"So, that's why you accepted Archer's invitation last night? Because you're lonely?"

"I'm not lonely," she said defiantly. "I have friends. Hobbies. I have a canary."

"You're lonely," he said. "That's why you went out with that snake."

"Are you deaf, Mr. McBride? I am not..." Emily frowned. "You think he's a snake?"

"Of course."

"That's what you've always thought?"

"Yes." Well, it was true if you figured "always" referred to yesterday evening, when Archer had sneaked up on Emily. "I tried to tell you that, but you wouldn't listen."

"You didn't try to tell me anything, except how to run my life." She cocked her head. "Pete Archer said you and he are best friends."

"Ha."

"He said you've known each other forever."

"Only if forever means a year working for the same brokerage firm, a long time back."

Emily puffed out a breath. "He lied to me." She looked at Jake. "You're right, by the way. He *is* a snake."

Jake's face darkened. "Did he—"

"Oh, I can handle men like Pete Archer." A smile ghosted across her lips. "When I was sixteen, one of my sisters dated a guy who was into karate. He taught me some great moves. I still remember them."

"Ah." Jake moistened his lips. "Let me get this straight. You, uh, you'd like to date. To meet some nice guys and go out. Is that it?"

What was the sense in trying to pretend otherwise? Jake McBride knew virtually everything about her now, from her shoe size to her sexless sex life.

"Yes."

"Well." He ran his hand through his hair again, turned away from her, paced back and forth, back and forth. "I've got it," he said, and swung towards her. "I know a lot of people. Some of them are nice guys, too. I'll introduce you."

"Oh, no. I couldn't ask you to—"

"You haven't asked, I've volunteered. Look, it's no big deal."

Emily collapsed into her chair. "What are you going to do," she said, with a nervous laugh, "go to a meeting and say, 'oh, by the way, my personal assistant would like to have a date this weekend'?"

Jake grinned at her. "My executive assistant," he said. "And I'll be subtle, I promise. For instance…well, I go to lots of cocktail parties. Business stuff. From now on, you'll go with me."

"Mr. McBride, really—"

"I'll introduce you as my good right hand, you'll circulate, network… Emily, don't look at me that way. It'll work, I know it will."

"It won't. I'm—I'm not good at this male-female thing, Mr. McBride."

"Jake."

"Jake," she said, because it was silly, really, to go on with such formality now. "Look, I appreciate your offer but it's pointless. I'll feel ridiculous."

"More ridiculous than you'd have felt if you'd left your number on that answering machine?"

Emily bit her lip. "Even if something came of it... For one thing, I don't know how to make small talk. "

"There's nothing to it. I'll teach you."

"Yes, but..." She waved a hand. "It's more than that. I don't dress right. My sisters used to tell me I had no idea of style."

Jake took a step back, looked her over slowly from head to toe. "We can take care of that with ease."

"I don't even know how to—" she blushed "—how to handle the, uh, the end of the evening thing."

"The...?" He colored. "Oh."

"Exactly. I mean, it was simple enough, last night. When your friend—"

"Archer's no friend of mine," Jake said grimly.

"The point is, when he, uh, when he tried to, you know, kiss me, I just put my hands up, the way you do in karate—"

Jake began to laugh. "I'd have given anything to have seen that."

"But—but if a man tried to kiss me and I wanted him to, I'd just mess it up. I'd—"

He felt his body tighten. "You mean you've never..." He cleared his throat, did a mental ten-count, reminded himself that Emily was a sparrow, not a thrush, and his lifelong preference was for songbirds. "Well," he said briskly, "never mind. I'll teach you everything you need to know. How to talk with a man. How to dress for him. How to make him want you, and only you."

"I don't know. It all seems to—so—"

"I'll teach you all you need to know, Emily." Jake's voice

roughened. "Including how to conduct yourself at the end of the evening."

Color swept into her face. "I can't believe I told you that," she whispered. "I feel so foolish!"

"I'll teach you," Jake said gently. He reached down, clasped her shoulders and lifted her to her feet. "You'll see. I'm an excellent teacher."

So saying, he bent his head, took Emily's face in his hands, and covered her mouth with his.

CHAPTER THREE

HIS mouth fit hers, perfectly.

His lips were warm, and dry, and pleasant. No tongue, Emily thought dazedly. None of that disgusting swapping spit stuff that the insufferable Pete Archer had tried last night.

Still, why was McBride kissing her? And why was she letting him? That was a better question.

Because he'd caught her by surprise. Why else? she told herself, and she put her hands against his chest and pulled back from his kiss.

"Mr. McBride," she said, a little breathlessly, "I really don't think—"

"Call me Jake," he said hoarsely but before she could call him anything, he put his arms around her, drew her against him and kissed her again.

The kiss wasn't the same.

She might have known it wouldn't be. His lips nudged hers, tugged at hers, moved against hers. And, when she tried to protest, to tell him there was no reason for them to kiss and certainly no reason to kiss like this, he used the moment against her and parted her lips with his.

Emily's hands came up, flattened against Jake's chest again.

No, she thought, no, please. No tongue, no spit, no awful wet kiss...

He didn't take the hint. He went right on with what he was doing, changing the rules, changing the kiss. What he was doing now—angling his mouth differently so that she had to tilt her head back as he slipped the tip of his tongue between her lips—what he was doing was—it was—

Oh, it was wonderful.

The feel of his arms around her. The hardness of his body against hers. The taste of his mouth. His hot mouth. His tongue. The glorious, mind-bending, mind-blowing heat and, yes, the wetness of his kiss...

Emily moaned. She curled her fingers into Jake's shirt, rose on her toes and pressed herself against him.

Was this what a kiss, a real kiss, was like? Was a man supposed to be able to turn a woman into a mindless, breathless, boneless creature with a kiss? Or did Jake know something other men didn't?

Not that Emily cared about any of the answers. She only knew that she wanted this feeling to go on forever.

Jake did, too.

It was crazy, to get so turned on by a kiss. But turned on, turned up, turned inside out was what he was, all right, and he was aching for more.

Emily wasn't just kissing him back, she was making the soft little noises a woman made when she wanted more. Her sweet body was pressing against his—grinding against his. Yes, indeed; there were curves under that boxy tweed jacket and bulky skirt, curves and warm, eager flesh.

And then she moved, and moaned, and Jake gave up thinking. He slid one hand down her spine, cupped her bottom, lifted her into the hardness of his arousal, knotted his hand in her skirt, pushed it up, stroked his hand along her thigh, her hot, silken thigh...

Told you, Archer's voice whispered smugly, way, way in the back of Jake's mind. *Didn't I say still waters run deep?*

Jake shoved Emily's skirt down, clasped her arms, tore his mouth from hers and stepped back. She swayed unsteadily, her eyes still shut, her lips rosy and parted.

Desire burned hot in his blood.

She wanted him, desired him, as much as he wanted her. And he wanted to assuage that desire. He wanted to reach out for her again, drag her back into his arms, carry her into his office, kick the door shut and rip away the tweed that hid her from his mouth and from his eyes…

But sanity prevailed. The last thing he wanted was an affair with his P.A. Uh, with his E.A. Hell, the last thing, absolutely the last thing, he wanted was an affair with a little brown sparrow who'd undoubtedly confuse sex with love.

Jake tried to speak, cleared his throat and tried again.

"You see?"

Emily blinked and opened her eyes. They were dark with passion and he felt himself teeter on the brink of that upside-down, inside-out feeling all over again.

He took another step back, shoved his hands into his trouser pockets and knotted them so he wouldn't be an idiot and reach for her.

"See what?" she croaked.

Jake tried for a nonchalant shrug. "I was just showing you that you don't have anything to worry about. I can teach you everything you need to know. It's not a problem."

Emily touched her fingers to her mouth. The simple action almost brought him to his knees.

"Not a problem at all," he said, and before she could respond, he went back into his office, fixed his tie and shirt, put on his jacket and coat, strode past her and headed out into the snowstorm for his lunch at the Oak Room…

And tried not to think about the kiss, or the fact that she'd been busy at her desk, fingers flying industriously over the keyboard as if the whole thing had never happened, as he went out the door.

Emily paused in her typing when Jake got back.

She looked up, greeted him politely and told him he'd find some faxes on his desk.

"Thank you," he said, and went straight into his office.

The door swung shut, and she almost collapsed with relief.

He wasn't going to mention what had happened. Thank God for that.

She'd worried that the kiss would affect their relationship. Foolish her. She should have known that it wouldn't. The kiss had meant nothing. Jake had, as he'd explained, been establishing his credentials, that was all.

Evidently, that was the way he always kissed a woman.

No wonder the twit wanted to keep him.

Any woman would. Well, not any woman. She wouldn't. Jake McBride wasn't her type at all, no more than she was his, and a kiss wouldn't change that. Not that he'd kissed her for that reason. To change her mind. To get her interested in him. No, it wasn't like that and a good thing, too, because she wasn't interested.

Emily looked at her computer screen. Her fingers had been busy but she'd been typing gibberish.

She took a breath, put her hands in her lap and folded them.

Okay. That was it. Enough. This was ridiculous, every bit of it, starting with Jake's nonsensical idea of introducing her to eligible men. Eligible for what? Was he going to run a Date My Assistant bureau?

All she'd wanted was to know what it was like to look forward to an occasional date but using your employer as a dating service was totally unacceptable. In the seven years since she'd come to New York, she'd heard of some strange employer-employee arrangements. She knew a secretary who baby-sat for her boss's golden retrievers on weekends, another who read all the books on the New York Times list, then wrote up one paragraph synopses for the man she worked for so he could sound as if he were well-read. She'd once met a P.A. whose boss baked him cookies. Awful cookies, but the poor guy had never worked up the courage to tell her so.

But a boss who got you dates?

No way.

That was what she'd tell Jake, if he brought up the subject

again. There wasn't a way in the world she was going to let her boss play matchmaker for...

"Emily?"

She looked up. Definitely, the kiss had meant nothing. Jake stood in the doorway between his office and hers. He looked the way he always did. Intense. Focused. Just a little bit forbidding.

The wings of hope fluttered in Emily's breast. Maybe she wouldn't have to tell him she was declining his offer. With luck, he might say it first.

"Yes, Mr. McBride?"

"Emily, I've given this some thought."

"Yes?"

"And I've decided you should leave."

The wings of hope faltered, folded and were still. "Leave?"

"That's what I said. I want you to go, right now."

"But..." He was firing her, because of that kiss? She pushed back her chair and stood up. "But it wasn't my idea."

Jake lifted his brows. "Obviously not."

"Then why..." *Why should I lose my job over your mistake?* "Why should I leave?"

"Look, I'm not going to debate this. I want you out of here, pronto."

Emily folded her arms. "I don't see any reason for this."

"No." Jake smiled tightly. "I didn't think you would."

"It's not fair. You've said, yourself, I'm good at my job."

"Of course you are. But whatever you're doing can wait until tomorrow."

"Now, just one minute, mister..." Emily frowned. "Tomorrow?"

"Nothing's so important that it can't be put off for a day."

"I don't..." She stared at him. "Are you telling me to leave early?"

Jake nodded. "I know you can't see the street from here—"

"No," she said, fumbling desperately for words, "uh, no, I can't. I don't have a window…"

"Exactly." Jake gave her a quick smile. "The snow's stopped and the streets are clear, but it's freezing out there and you know what happens to the subways when the temperature drops to zero."

"What?" she said stupidly. "I mean, yes. Yes, I know…"

"What's wrong?"

"Nothing," she said quickly. "I mean…well, I thought—only for a minute, you understand—I thought…"

She couldn't say it. What an idiot she was, thinking he'd fire her because of a silly kiss. He was a man who kissed women all the time, kissed them until they were clinging to him as if he were a lifeline and they were drowning in his arms.

"…I thought the temperature was supposed to stay in the mid-thirties," she said briskly. "Thanks for the warning."

Oh, yes. Most definitely, the sooner she was out of here, the better. This had been the weirdest day of her life. Thankfully, she'd come to her senses. McBride had, too. He hadn't even mentioned the Introduce Emily Around campaign. Better still, she had the feeling he'd never mention it again.

Life was still good, she thought, and smiled brightly in Jake's direction.

"Thank you again, sir. I appreciate your concern." She shut off her computer, cleared off her desk, got her things from the closet and sat down to put on her socks and boots.

"Emily."

She looked up. He was leaning against the wall, eyes hooded, arms folded, watching her.

"Do you need me?"

"Do I… do I need you?"

"All you have to do is tell me you want me, Emily. You know that."

"I don't." She spoke quickly, too quickly, she knew, but

what kind of question was that to ask? Here she'd thought the kiss wouldn't stand in the way of their continuing to have a good working relationship, and then he'd asked if she—

"Of course, if you're sure you can get those boots on by yourself…"

The boots. Oh the stupid boots. Emily wanted to laugh but she didn't dare. Instead, she gave him another bright smile.

"I'll be fine, thank you, Mr. McBride."

"You're sure."

"I'm positive."

Jake nodded. "In that case, I'll see you in the morning."

"Certainly, Mr. McBride."

"Jake. I thought we agreed on that."

"Jake," she said, and beamed at him again. "I'll try and remember that, sir."

"'Sir' and 'Jake' don't go together, Emily."

He smiled. She smiled. She was tired of smiling. Her lips felt as if they'd been stretched on a rack.

Jake strolled into his office, stopped, and swung towards her. "Oh, Emily?"

"Mr. Mc…? I mean, Yes, Jake?"

"While you're remembering things, remember not to wear tweed tomorrow."

Her face creased in puzzlement. "I beg your pardon?"

"Tweed," he said patiently, jerking his chin towards her. "That's what that stuff you're wearing is called, isn't it?"

Emily glanced down at herself. "Well, no," she said slowly, "actually, it's not. Tweed is nubby and coarse. This is just a heavy wool worsted—"

"How about silk?" Jake said, before she could treat him to a dissertation on fabrics.

"How about it?" she said, looking at him with caution.

Jake sighed. He was starting to regret the deal they'd made. First, for reasons he couldn't figure out, he'd teased her about helping her with the boots and he'd seen that she'd taken him seriously. Now she was staring at him as if he'd asked her if she had anything in her closet made of chain mail.

"Silk," he said. "You know, that soft stuff made by silk moths?"

"Silk worms, sir. Yes. Yes, I do."

"A dress?"

"A suit. But—"

Jake sighed again. "A suit. Well, that figures. Okay. Wear it tomorrow."

Emily furrowed her brow. "Why?"

"Because," he said, through his teeth, "tweed—"

"Wool worsted."

"Whatever. It won't go over, tomorrow night."

"Tomorrow…?"

"Internet Resources is giving a cocktail party. You penciled it into my appointment book."

"I remember, sir. Jake. But what does that have to do with me?"

"Emily, Emily, what a short memory you have. Our plan? For you to meet men? You'll go with me." He smiled. "Actually, there's an even better thing tonight but…" His voice trailed off. But, you're not dressed for it, he'd almost said, but why hurt her feelings? "But, considering the weather, I wouldn't want to see you having to ride the subway all the way to… Where is it you live again? Brooklyn?"

"Tribeca," Emily said stiffly. "Mr. McBride—"

"Tribeca," he repeated, as if she'd said she lived in Outer Mongolia. "Too bad. Tonight's affair—"

"What affair?"

"The one I've been talking about. Cocktails and dinner, for United Broadcasting. I thought they might call it off, because of the weather, but I spoke with one of the V.P.'s a while ago and he said—"

"No!"

"Yes. I just told you, the Veep said—"

"No, I am not going with you tomorrow night."

"Of course you are. That's the plan, remember? You'll network, I'll introduce you around—"

"Absolutely not."

"What do you mean, absolutely not?" Jake straightened up and walked towards her. "We agreed this was a good plan."

"Well, it isn't." Emily tucked her socks into a desk drawer and quickly pulled on her boots. No socks; she wasn't going to leave herself open to that problem again. She stood up, put on her coat and buttoned it. "I've thought about your idea, Mr....Jake. And I just don't see myself meeting men that way."

"Ah," Jake said, and folded his arms. "Of course. You'd rather meet them through ads in magazines."

She could feel color rising into her cheeks. "Whatever I choose to do, it isn't your concern."

"Meaning, I should mind my own business."

"Meaning, I'm an adult. I can take care of myself."

"Listen, Emily—"

"Why should it matter to you, who I go out with?"

Why, indeed? "Because I'm your employer. I'm your friend."

"We have never been friends, sir," Emily said politely. "That's as it should be. You're my employer, as you said. I am your employee. That has always been the extent of our relationship."

She was right. She was his P.A. His E.A. She wasn't his friend. But, dammit, that didn't mean he wasn't concerned about her welfare.

"That doesn't mean I'm not concerned about your welfare," Jake said with self-righteous indignation. "I'd much rather know the men you date than worry about you meeting up with the Boston Strangler."

"Oh, for goodness sakes... Look, Mr. McBride. Jake." Emily put her hands on her hips and tried her best not to glare. "You're blowing this out of all proportion. I don't go out with men."

"You went out with Archer."

"Only because I was angry at you."

"Well, that's certainly reassuring," Jake said, his words ripe with sarcasm. "You don't go out with men but you went out with this one because you were mad at me. That's a heck of a way to pick a date, isn't it?"

"I just told you, I don't have dates!"

"Then, what were you doing with *GOTHAM* magazine?"

"Reading it," she said sharply. "You do understand the concept, don't you?"

Jake's eyes narrowed. "Don't try and play smart with me, Miss Taylor. You know damn well what I'm talking about." He reached past her, snatched the magazine from the wastebasket and waved it in front of her. "You were in the process of leaving your name and phone number at the local loony bin when I stopped you!"

"The local…" Emily laughed. "You're being ridiculous," she said and started past him, but Jake snagged her by the elbow.

"Ridiculous? When hardly a day goes by there isn't something in the paper about a woman getting robbed, raped and murdered? When this city's full of perverts?"

"Let go of me."

"You want to be a statistic? You want the cops to call me and ask me to come identify the body?"

"You're not just being ridiculous, Mr. McBride. You're stark-raving mad."

Hell. Maybe he was. She wanted to go out with the reincarnation of Vlad the Impaler, was it his business? No, it was not.

"Okay, then." Jake took his hand from her arm with deliberate exaggeration. "Answer the Personals. Pick up guys on street corners, for all I care."

"Thank you. It's good to know I have your permission."

"Go out with guys you just met because you're pissed off at me."

"An excellent idea," Emily said, eyes flashing as she tried to step past him.

"Date any Tom, Dick or Harry who comes up to you on the subway and says 'Hi, honey, how about a movie?'"

"I would never," she said icily, "accept a date from a man I didn't know."

"Except for last night," Jake snarled.

"Except for last night…but then, why would I assume that my boss would introduce me to an octopus?"

"Is that what he was?" Jake's eyes glittered. He took hold of Emily's shoulders and propelled her backwards. "What did that son of a bitch do to you? Tell me. I'll hunt him down and beat the crap out of him."

"I told you, he didn't do anything. And I don't need a protector!"

"You're right." He slapped his hands on either side of her, palms flat against the wall. "What you need is a keeper."

He was only inches from her, so close that he could see a tiny muscle just beside her mouth. It was moving in time with her heartbeat, fast and furious, and he wondered what would happen if he put his lips against it, if he'd somehow absorb the race of her blood into his.

"Jake," she said, in a low voice.

His eyes went to hers. She was looking at him as if she'd never seen him before and maybe she hadn't. He felt like a stranger in his own body, a man wanting to do things he knew were crazy.

This was his assistant. This was Emily Taylor, she of the efficient brain and unremarkable body. Except, he knew that body wasn't unremarkable at all. He wanted to prove that to her, to put his hands into her hair, pull it free of the clip and let it spill like dark silk through his fingers. He wanted to unbutton her coat, lift her skirt, seek out her heat.

Most of all, more than any of that, he wanted to kiss her again.

"Emily," he said huskily, and his gaze dropped to her mouth. "Emily…"

She moved fast, ducked under his arm and reached for the doorknob. But Jake was quicker. He grabbed her arm and swung her around.

"Look," he said, in what he hoped was a tone of reason, "try and see this from my angle, okay? I, ah, I feel some responsibility for you, Emily. You work for me. You don't have any family in the city."

"How do you know that?"

Because he'd pulled out her job application again and read it thoroughly, that was why. All of a sudden, he'd wanted to know her age, her marital status, as much as he could find out about her. It was perfectly logical, too. A man had to research his subject before he could play matchmaker.

"You told me so, when you applied here. You said you were from Rochester. Right?"

"Right," she said, a little grudgingly. "But that doesn't mean—"

"Look, I feel guilty about last night. If I hadn't introduced you to Archer, if I hadn't made you so angry at me…"

"It isn't your fault." She sighed, looked up, managed a quick smile. "What I told you was the truth. I'm an adult, and I take full responsibility for my actions. Accepting Archer's dinner invitation was foolish. I'm to blame, not you. As for the personal ads… You're right. They're not for me."

Jake smiled. The tendrils of hair he'd noticed this morning were still clinging to her temples. He reached out, touched one, watched as it curled around his finger.

"Good. I'd hate to end up paying a visit to each of those guys in that listing."

Emily's eyes widened. "Why would you do that?"

He shrugged, caught the curl between his thumb and index fingers, let it slide against his skin.

"To warn them that they'd have to answer to me, if they tried any funny stuff."

She laughed. Her whole face lit up, when she laughed. How come he'd never noticed that before?

"Just what I need," she said. "A bodyguard."

"Yeah," Jake said. His gaze dropped to her mouth, then returned to her eyes. "That's what you need, all right."

"Well, you can stop worrying. I promise, I won't go out with anybody who describes himself as H, S, and S."

"H, S, and S?"

"Handsome, sexy and successful. I figure it's only a matter of time before those ads are all initials and numbers. You know, H, S and S, B and B, ISO for B, S and S... Jake? What are you doing?"

Slipping the clip from her hair, that's what he was doing. He felt her shudder as he moved his fingers lightly against her scalp.

"Is this natural?"

"Is what natural?" she whispered. Her mouth was too dry for anything but a whisper.

"This." He took a handful of her hair, let it sift though his hand. "The color. What do you call it?"

"What do you call the color of my hair?" Emily laughed nervously. "Brown. As in, 'mouse.'"

"Brown, as in 'sparrow,'" Jake murmured, and smiled. "I like it." He leaned forward, took a sniff. "I like the smell, too. What is it?"

Emily could feel her heart, pounding in her throat. "It's—it's just shampoo. Whatever was on sale last week."

"Nice. Smells like sunshine and flowers."

"Mr. McBride. Jake. I really have to leave, if I want to miss the worst of the subway rush—"

"What about the others?"

"The other what?" It was hard to talk. She wanted to shut her eyes, lean into his stroking hand, draw his scent of cold air and hot male deep into her lungs. "What others? The shampoos? I don't know. I only buy whatever is—"

"The other guys you'll date." Jake shifted his weight. His body brushed hers. She felt soft. So soft. So wonderfully, marvelously soft. "What about them?"

"What *about* them?" she said, because the only way to respond to a question that made no sense was with an answer that made no sense. How could it, when she was feeling so strange? So warm. So liquid. So...

"The guys you'll go out with. Those you'll meet that I don't know. How am I going to know they're harmless?"

Emily stiffened. Jake McBride was leaning over her, smelling her hair, stroking her cheek, breathing in the same air she was breathing, and he was asking her about the men she intended to date?

How on earth had she let him maneuver her into such a situation?

Emily scowled, put a hand in the center of Jake's chest and shoved him away.

"That's easy," she said crisply. "You won't have to worry about a thing because I won't be dating anybody."

He blinked. "What?"

"You heard me." She dug into her coat pocket, took out a sensible wool scarf and wrapped it around her neck. Then she dug into the other pocket, took out a pair of sensible woolen gloves and pulled them on. "I've rethought things, Mr. McBride."

"Jake," he said automatically, while he stared at her and tried to figure out how he'd ended up playing with Emily Taylor's very proper hair.

"Mr. McBride," Emily corrected politely. "I really do think it's advisable to maintain decorum in the office, don't you?"

"No. I mean, yes. Calling me by my first name doesn't change office decorum. Actually, I don't think I know another secretary who calls her boss 'Mr.'"

"I am not your secretary, Mr. McBride."

"I know that. I only meant... You're in a very contrary frame of mind lately, Emily."

"I don't think so."

"Well, I do. And, as you've just pointed out, I'm your boss and you're my employee. If I say you're contrary, you're contrary."

She smiled politely. "Whatever you say, sir."

"Dammit, this is ridiculous. Calling me 'sir,' and 'Mr.' I've got a good mind to—"

The door squeaked open. "Jake?"

Jake froze. He looked up, past Emily, and groaned.

"Brandi," he said tonelessly, and took a couple of steps back.

Brandi slipped into the office and put her arms around his neck. "Jake," she whispered, "have you been trying to avoid me?"

Did flies avoid flypaper?

Jake reached up, grasped her wrists and drew them to her sides. "What are you doing here, Brandi?"

"I came to see you. To ask why you've been ignoring my calls."

She smiled up at him, or pouted. One or the other. It was hard for him to tell. She had what she called bee-stung lips. Collagen stung, was more like it. Whatever, Jake wanted no part of her lips or her.

"Brandi," he said kindly, "I've already explained that what you and I had is—"

"Don't say it! It isn't. It can't be."

"Brandi..."

"I reserved a corner table at Alfredo's. We can have a nice quiet dinner and talk things over."

"No," Jake said firmly. "I'm sorry, Brandi, but there's no point in that."

"Of course there is."

"There isn't."

"There is."

"Well," Emily said brightly, "it's getting late, Mr. McBride. And you know what you said about the cold. So, if you don't mind—"

"You're right," Jake said quickly. "It is getting late."

"Exactly. Which is why I'm just going to—"

"Wait right there, Emily. Don't move a muscle."

Jake hurried into his office. The women's eyes met. Emily's lips turned up in a faint smile. Brandi's turned down, or would have, if she'd been able to move them. Enough, Emily thought, and reached for the door...

"I'm ready," Jake said.

She turned and looked at Jake. He'd put on his jacket, his coat and gloves. Smiling, he reached for her hand. She pulled it back. He trapped it with his leather-gloved fingers, wound them through hers.

"What are you doing?" she hissed.

"We have to leave now or we'll be late." He smiled, but his eyes flashed a warning. "You know how Donovan is about people being late."

"Who?"

"Donovan. The chairman."

"What chairman? Jake, what—"

He bent his head, silenced Emily by brushing his mouth gently over hers. Then he looked at Brandi, who was staring at him with a stricken expression on her perfectly made-up face. Two perfect tears rose in her eyes and trickled artistically down her cheeks.

"You and this—this creature? You don't mean it."

"Ah," Jake said, and smiled at Emily. "But I do."

Emily would have protested but how could she? Jake had already drawn her into his arms so he could kiss her, just the way he had the last time, until she felt her toes curl inside the too-tight boots.

CHAPTER FOUR

WHO would show up at a party in snowy Manhattan on a frigid January night?

Everybody who'd been invited, or so it seemed.

Emily had expected to see ten or twenty lost souls with nothing better to do than attend the UBS celebration. But when the elevator doors slid open to the Sunset Room on the fortieth floor of the Ascot Towers, she could see that even the corridor was alive with people.

Famous people. People whose faces lit up TV and movie screens from coast to coast...

People dressed for the occasion.

Emily touched an uneasy hand to her dampness-frizzed hair, glanced down at her sensible coat and equally sensible boots, and blanched.

"Uh-oh," she whispered.

Jake, who figured the "uh oh" was an exclamation of delight, put his hand lightly in the small of her back and moved her forward.

"See?" he said softly. "Aren't you glad you let me talk you into coming?"

No, she wasn't. She was as out of place here as she'd been at that long-ago high school prom, where she'd showed up in a full-skirted, pale blue satin gown with puffy sleeves and a bow when every other girl in the room had been wearing clingy, slinky black silk.

As for "talk..." The man didn't know the meaning of the word. He'd hustled her out of the office, into a cab and towards Fifth Avenue so fast that it had made her head spin. All the "talk" had been hers. She'd demanded he let her out of the taxi so she could go home but Jake had ignored her protests. He hadn't "talked" her into coming here, he'd shanghaied her.

Still, Emily had to admit, if reluctantly, that being here might have its uses, now that Jake had promoted her. There were more business contacts just in the corridor than she'd ever imagined a person could find in one place, and from the "hello's" and "how are you's" Jake was exchanging as they moved slowly towards the Sunset Room, her boss knew every last one of—

"Jake. Great to see you."

"You, too, Thad." Jake smiled and looked at Emily. "Thad, I'd like you to meet Emily Taylor, my executive assistant. Emily, this is Thaddeus Jennett."

"Miss Taylor."

Emily blinked. "Thad" was none other than the handsome, debonair anchor on UBS's top-rated evening news show.

"Nice to meet you," she said, and took the hand Thad extended to her.

"We'll catch up to you later," Jake said, taking Emily's elbow, "just as soon as we find the checkroom and get rid of these coats."

Get rid of these coats? Emily clutched her collar in a death grip. She felt out of place enough as it was. The last thing she was going to do was peel off her coat and stand around like a plain gray goose in a sea of sexy swans.

"I don't want to find the checkroom," she hissed.

But Jake didn't hear her. He was stopping again, introducing her again, to the star in the newest UBS romantic comedy, then to the guy's publicist. Emily said hello, did her best to make small talk and tried not to wonder what people must be thinking.

"Not so bad, is it?" Jake whispered as he drew her forward.

"Why didn't you tell me this would be so—so dressed up?"

Jake lifted an eyebrow. "Let's see. One, you didn't ask. Two, bringing you with me was a last-minute decision."

"That's an interesting way to put it," Emily said coolly.

"Three," he said, ignoring the interruption, "you didn't want to come, anyway. Four...four, would it have mattered? Do you own anything that would have worked tonight?"

Emily's mouth turned down. "That's none of your business."

"I didn't say it was. You were the one who raised the issue. Besides—"

"Jake!"

The shriek was loud enough to shatter glass. A tall, exquisite blonde hurled herself into Jake's arms.

"Jake, lover, is it true you and Brandi are..." The blonde drew back, made a face and slid her hand across her throat.

Jake grinned. "Hello, Crystal, news travels quickly in this town."

"Good news, you mean," the blonde replied, and looped her arm through his. "Come get me a drink and tell me how I can help you recover from the loss."

"A little later, maybe. Let me get rid of my coat, first..." He paused, frowned, and looked at Emily. "Sorry," he muttered.

"No problem," Emily said sweetly, and held out her hand. "I'm Emily Taylor, Mr. McBride's executive assistant. How do you do, Miss...?"

"How nice," the blonde said, in a tone that made it clear it wasn't, and turned her attention back to Jake. "Darling, I'm so glad to see you! Honestly, it's been so long..."

The sexy voice droned on. Emily felt her face turning hot. She'd been dismissed, totally and completely, as only one woman can dismiss another. Well, so what? She was here as Jake's business associate, not as his date. Exchanging names with someone like this—this person wasn't important. It wouldn't do a thing for her career, or for McBride Investments...

Oh, who was she kidding?

Never mind careers. What about egos? She had one, even though she hardly ever let it show its face to the world, and it was her ego that was warning her what the rest of the evening would be like.

She was here as a stand-in for Brandi, but that was a joke. The blonde, draped over Jake's arm with the determination of a boa constrictor on its prey, was determined to be Brandi's successor. She was also a harbinger of what lay ahead.

Women would swarm around Jake like bees around honeysuckle. They'd all be beautiful. They'd have perfect hair, perfect smiles, perfect makeup, perfect bodies. Her prom, all over again. She'd be the plain-but-brainy wallflower on the sidelines, whose date had wandered off, smiling until her face hurt, pretending it didn't matter that she was alone, that no boy had come near her...

No. It would be worse than her prom. This was real life, not high school. And Jake, gorgeous, sexy Jake, would laud her as his executive assistant—his sexless executive assistant—and then flirt with every woman in the place except her.

She didn't care, though. He could do what he wanted, with whatever woman he wanted. She really didn't...

Emily turned on her heel, pushed her way through the still-crowded corridor, made her way to the elevators and stabbed the call button.

She didn't have to be here. She didn't have to spend the evening with her boss. Her day began at nine and ended at five, thank you very much, unless you counted the endless overtime she put in and never, ever bothered mentioning to Jake.

Well, he was in for a surprise.

Emily pushed the button again. Where was that miserable elevator? You'd think, in a hotel like this, one would come when you wanted it.

Jake would have to learn that she had a life of her own. That she couldn't trot along behind him like a well-trained puppy. That when she said no, no was what she meant. No more letting him dictate commands, or bait her into dizzy arguments she couldn't win. She wouldn't permit it. She wouldn't let Jake get under her skin...

Or touch it. Stroke it, with his hand. With his lips...

"Dammit!" Emily growled, and slammed the call button again.

As if in response, the doors slid open and disgorged a carful of laughing, chattering party guests. Emily tapped her foot impatiently, waited until the car emptied, slipped inside...

"What do you think you're doing?"

Jake suddenly loomed in the space between the slowly closing doors. She could see only his face, dark with annoyance, and his hand as he jammed it between the doors, forced them open and stepped into the car with her.

The doors swished shut. Suddenly, the car felt small. Very small, and very, very airless but there wasn't a way in the world she'd let him know that.

"I'm going home," she said briskly, and pressed the lobby button.

"Going home, or running away?"

"You're wasting your time if you think you'll bait me into going back, Mr. McBride. You want to think I'm running away? Fine. Think it."

"Don't be silly." Jake spoke calmly. So calmly that she wanted to slug him. "We just got here."

"So?"

"So, I'm not ready to leave."

"I'm not asking you to." Emily slapped the button again. Why was the damned elevator moving so slowly? "In fact, I don't want you to leave. Not when you're obviously having such a good time."

Jake's dark brows lifted. "Interesting. Who'd have suspected the formidably efficient Ms. Taylor has normal female instincts?''

"I've no idea what you're talking about.''

"Could it be,'' he said, with just a hint of smug satisfaction, "that you're jealous of Crystal?''

"Is that her name?'' Emily folded her arms and stared straight ahead at the blinking lights on the control panel. "You sure it isn't Brandi the Second?'' The elevator came to a stop. The doors slid open but no one got on. After a minute, the doors shut and the downward journey resumed. "Your companions are difficult to tell apart, considering that they're always tall, leggy, and brain-dead.''

Jake laughed. "You *are* jealous.''

"Jealous? Of your women?''

"I don't have 'women.' Anyway, I've known Crystal for years.''

"You can know her for centuries, for all I care. Dammit, what is with this elevator? Why doesn't it move?''

"It is moving,'' Jake said. "If anything, it's moving too fast.''

And, just like that, he reached out and hit the Stop button. The car lurched to a halt. Emily staggered and landed against Jake's chest. His arms went around her but she jerked away.

"What do you think you're doing?'' she demanded.

Jake leaned back against the wood-paneled wall and folded his arms. "We came here so you could network.''

"You came here to network.'' Emily glowered at the closed doors. "I came here so you could save yourself from a fate worse than death.''

"Yeah.'' He gave a sigh of apology. "Listen, about that. I'm really sorry but—''

"But,'' Emily said coldly, "that's okay. It turns out I *did* network. I met three people. Four, if I expand the list to include life-size mannequins with improbable names.''

She reached towards the Stop button but Jake's hand shot out and clamped around her wrist.

"There are lots more people to meet, if you're going to be my exec."

"I thought you brought me here to meet eligible men."

"Yeah, that was part of the plan." Jake's jaw tightened. "But you changed your mind… Didn't you?"

"I've changed it again," she said coldly. "Yes, I want to meet men. The more the better."

"In that case, let's go back to the party."

"No."

"Emily, don't be an idiot. That party's loaded with candidates."

"Oh, I'm sure it is. Crystal-clones are probably everywhere!"

"I'm not talking about Crystal, I'm talking about…" Jake scowled and let go of Emily's hand. What *was* he talking about? If she wanted to meet men, that was her business. But if she was serious about being his exec, that was his business. She had to start spending some time with him at functions like this one. That was reasonable, wasn't it? "Look, we won't stay long."

"I stayed too long, already."

"Will you stop being so foolish?"

"I am not being foolish. I am being sensible."

"The hell you are. You want to meet men? Well, there they are, a dozen floors above us. Men. Young, old, in between. Fat ones, thin ones, lawyers, bankers and corporate types, all arrayed for your pleasure like hors d'oeuvres on a buffet table."

"I'm not interested," Emily said sharply. "Can't you get that through your thick head? I want to meet men, not have you play go-between."

"You sure as hell need somebody as a go-between! When you search for dates on your own—"

"I do not search for dates!"

"—when you run your own campaign, the guys you come up with are creeps."

"All right," Emily said furiously, "this has gone far enough."

Jake grabbed her and swung her towards him as she reached for the Stop button. His eyes had turned a dark, forbidding green. "Okay. We'll forget whether or not you're in the mood to start behaving like a real woman. Let's stick to business. I promoted you yesterday. You want to be my exec? Start acting like one."

"I will. I *have,* for months now. I do your research. I soothe your clients. I see to it that your office runs without a hiccup. But I *don't* have to subject myself to—to standing around on the sidelines in a room filled with overdressed, overmade up females who think life begins and ends with you."

"Listen to me, Emily. We're going upstairs. You're going to that party, by my side."

"What for? You don't need me there. I'm not Jacob McBride, Super-Macho Investment Broker. And before you tell yourself that's a compliment, it isn't."

"P.A's go home at five. E.A's network. That's why you're going to smile, shake some hands, let me introduce you around." Jake smiled through his teeth. "Or I can take you downstairs, put you in a taxi, and you can go back to being my secretary and my personal assistant. Your choice."

Emily stared at him. "Why are you doing this?" she finally asked. "I mean, it's just a party. You really think I should go to these things, okay. I will. But I don't see what's so important about tonight."

Actually, he didn't, either. Yeah, it would help if she met some of the UBS people but it wasn't vital. Keeping her at his side tonight was going to cramp his style; he'd be so busy making sure she didn't make a run for the elevators or bolt for the fire stairs that he'd probably spend more time concentrating on her than on the people he'd come to see.

And she was right, about not being dressed for the occasion. She'd look out of place. Well, so what? Crystal was a sight every man in the room would enjoy but she wasn't bright, the way Emily was. She didn't have Emily's sense of fun. And she'd never drive him crazy, making him want to throttle her one minute and kiss her the next...

Jake frowned, took an involuntary step back.

"I told you the reason," he said brusquely. "Now, do you want the promotion or don't you?"

The cool, insolent look on Jake's handsome face was infuriating. Emily debated the wisdom of telling the mighty McBride what he could do with both the job and the promotion, thought better of it, and lifted her chin.

"I really don't like you, Mr. McBride," she said coldly. "But I do like my job." She undid the belt at the waistline of her coat, snatched the wool scarf from her throat, the wool gloves from her hands, tucked them into her pockets and took the coat off. "Very well. I'm ready."

She said it as if she'd just agreed to an evening of root canal, Jake thought. And she looked about as eager.

He sighed, took her coat and let it fall to the floor.

Emily's eyes widened. "Hey," she said, "what do you think you're—"

Jake reached out and tugged the clip from her hair. The damp, snowy weather had turned it to a mass of curls; freed of constraint, they tumbled around her face and to her shoulders like a frothy mass of coffee-colored silk.

"Are you crazy? Give me that clip!"

Jake dropped the clip in his pocket, then ran his fingers through her hair.

"You *are* crazy!" Emily slapped at his hands. "Stop that!"

"You have beautiful hair," he said. "Why don't you make the most of it?"

"What do you know about it? Curls aren't professional."

"Dressing like your grandmother is?"

"You don't know anything about my grandmother, either. Jake. Jake! What are you doing?"

"Getting rid of this horse-blanket," Jake said grimly, as he tugged her suit jacket from her shoulders and dumped it on top of the coat that lay at her feet.

"Dammit, Jake..."

"It's a cocktail party," he said, as he undid the first button of her blouse, "not a wake. You're the one who pointed out that you weren't dressed right." Emily grabbed at his hand as he started working on the second button but he shrugged her off. "We'll do what little we can. Let your hair down, get rid of that jacket, open a few buttons..."

"Hey," a voice called, from somewhere outside the elevator, "anybody stuck in there?"

People, Emily thought desperately, people near enough to save her. But save her from what? It was hard to concentrate, when she was so furious at Jake...

...when Jake's fingers were at the next tiny button on her blouse.

Emily grabbed his wrist. "Stop it!"

He didn't stop. He kept going, opening buttons, muttering that it was time she stepped into the twenty-first century and let herself look like a woman, until she glanced down at herself and saw the first hint of...

"Lace?"

Jake's voice cracked. He looked up. Emily did, too. Their eyes met, and she could see that his were no longer cold and dark but a deep, hot emerald. Her heart did a strange two-step before lodging in her throat.

"Lace," he said again, very softly, "under all those layers of wool."

"I happen to like..." Emily licked her lips. Jake followed the movement of her tongue with an almost unholy fascination. She took a step back but there was nowhere to go; her shoulders hit the wall of the car. "I happen to like lace," she said, in a voice that sounded as if she were a marathon runner approaching the finish line. "Besides, what I wear under the wool is none of your—"

"Shut up, Emily," Jake said, and kissed her.

It was a gentle kiss, hardly a kiss at all. Only their mouths met, his moving over hers in soft, exploratory touches.

And then he groaned, or maybe she did. The only thing Emily knew for sure was that, suddenly, she was in his arms.

His kiss changed, then, became the kiss of a conqueror, hungry and rapacious, demanding surrender. And even as she told herself not to give in, she curled her arms around his neck, opened her mouth to his and kissed him back.

Jake gathered her tightly against him. She swept her hands into his hair, tugged his head down and lifted herself to him. He pressed her back against the wall. She moaned. He was so hard. So strong. So aroused and so completely, magnificently male.

He wanted her.

Wanted her, as much as she wanted him.

His arms offered no escape and she desired none. This, this was what she yearned for. Jake's lips, plundering hers. His tongue, in her mouth. His erection, against her belly.

Emily whimpered, twisted in his arms, wanting something more now, wanting it with sweet desperation. Jake pulled her blouse out from the waistband of her skirt, swept his hands beneath it and up to her breasts. He groaned her name, moved his thumbs against her lace-covered nipples and she sobbed with the ecstasy of it.

This, yes. This was what she ached for. Jake's touch. The pads of his thumbs moving, like that. Just like that, stroking her there. The curling ribbon of fire that lanced from her breasts to her belly. The answering tug of liquid heat between her thighs.

"Emily," Jake said thickly.

He drew back. She moaned, refused to let him go until she realized he only wanted enough room to undo the rest of her buttons.

"Let me," he said, "Emily, let me..."

"Yes," she whispered, against his mouth, "Jake, yes..."

Off in the distance, an alarm bell began to ring. Emily didn't hear it. The beat of her heart, the sexy-sweet rasp of Jake's whispers, drowned out everything else as he eased her blouse open.

"Beautiful." His eyes, so hot and dark, locked onto hers as he ran the roughened tip of his index finger along the soft, warm curve of flesh that rose above the lace of her camisole. "Such a beautiful little sparrow."

He bent his head, let the tip of his tongue follow the same path as his finger and she cried out, arched towards him...

Emily's shoulder hit the Stop switch. The car lurched into motion. After a few seconds, so did her brain.

She was in an elevator in the Ascot Towers. It was heading up, towards a floor filled with people. And she was half-undressed, making love with her boss.

"Jake!" She shoved against his shoulders, tugged at his hair. "Jake! The elevator. The car's going up!"

Right, Jake thought dazedly, and slipped his hand under her chemise. Everything was going up. And the ground was shifting under his feet.

"Stop it," Emily hissed, into his ear. "Do you hear me? Stop!"

Stop? How was he supposed to...

"Jake!"

Emily pounded her fists against his back. He blinked, looked up, and realized that it wasn't the ground shifting, it was the elevator. It was rising, and fast. Thirty, said the panel indicator lights. Thirty-one. Thirty-two...

"Hell!"

Jake grabbed Emily's jacket from the floor, draped it around her shoulders, draped her coat over that. He ran his hands through her hair, through his hair, tugged at his tie, his shirt...

The elevator stopped. The doors slid open and a small sea of faces peered at them.

"Hey, McBride," a male voice said, "you guys okay? This thing must have been stuck for twenty minutes."

Jake peeled his lips back from his teeth. "We're fine."

"Fine," Emily croaked.

Fine? Jake smothered a groan. She was as pale as a ghost; he could feel her trembling in the curve of his arm.

"Miss Taylor," he said, "my, ah, my assistant. She, uh, she has a touch of claustrophobia…"

"Claustrophobia," Emily said, and smiled brightly.

Jake tightened his hold, led her through the little crowd, down the hall and towards the party. Halfway there, she dug in her heels and balked.

"I can't go in there looking like this," she hissed.

He nodded. Of course she couldn't. Neither could he. What they could do was turn around, get back into the elevator, stop at the reservation desk in the lobby and take a room for the night…

Oh, hell.

He cleared his throat, looked around, saw the discreet signs for the lounges, and pointed her towards the ladies' room.

Emily disappeared through the door. Jake stumbled into the men's room. It was empty, but he wasn't taking any chances. He went into a stall, locked the door, took off his coat and hung it up. He straightened his shirt, his tie, his suit jacket, checked out his fly. Then he sagged against the wall and tried to figure out what had just happened.

Actually, what hadn't happened, no thanks to him. If the elevator hadn't started moving, he'd have made love to Emily right then and there. Made love to a sparrow, when there was a nest full of brightly plumed chicks just aching to be plucked only seconds away.

He groaned and rubbed his hands over his face.

Never mind that, he thought grimly, forget the bird analogy. The bottom line was that no man with even half a brain in his head got involved with his secretary. Okay, so Emily was his executive assistant, not his secretary. Whatever she was, he had to be out of his mind, even sniffing the air in her direction.

He hissed with frustration.

An intelligent man did not get involved with a woman who worked for him, even if she looked like a goddess, which Emily most certainly did not. Just imagining the repercussions of such a relationship were staggering. The sexual harassment charges. And even if there weren't any, the emotional complications…

He was a civilized man. He ended relationships in ways that were bloodless. Jake thought of Brandi and winced. Okay. Relatively bloodless. And that would never be possible if he had an affair with Emily. It was bad enough to have a woman stalking him like the ghost of Hamlet's father but if that woman worked for him, there'd be no avoiding her at all. She'd be there, all day, every day, sniveling into a hanky and giving him damp-eyed, woeful looks.

No way. No, no, no. A smart man didn't ever mix business with pleasure, and Jake had always been smart, when it came to both.

He put his coat over his arm, unlocked the stall door, walked to the sink and turned on the cold water.

Emily was an excellent secretary. An excellent associate. He had no intention of losing her and he would, if he let his gonads get in the way.

He draped his coat over a chair, splashed cold water over his face.

Okay. So he'd done something stupid but the damage wasn't irreversible. He knew the reason things had gotten out of hand, in the elevator.

It was the shock of seeing that white lace.

"Hey," he said softly, to his reflection in the mirror over the sink, "who expects to see Mary Poppins wearing white lace?"

Not him. Definitely, not him.

He took a towel from the stack neatly piled on the marble countertop, dried his hands and face, then tossed it aside.

That was all of it. The unexpected glimpse of lace. And, yeah, that cloud of silken curls. And all right, the surprising roundness, the feel of her breasts. The smell of her skin. The taste of her mouth. The way she'd responded to him, all that heat and fire...

"Dammit, McBride!"

Was he crazy? He was supposed to be reminding himself of how foolish it would be to take things even a step further; instead, he was turning himself on.

Okay. That was it. What had happened tonight was the start and finish of his relationship with Emily.

She'd be disappointed.

He knew she would be, Jake thought, and sighed. After what had happened just now, Emily had to figure this night would end with him in her bed. He'd have to reason with her, make her see that even though he'd like that, too, it was out of the question. It would only make for trouble. She'd just have to understand.

There was no sense letting her think that things could progress between them.

Jake nodded at his reflection. "She'll have to understand," he murmured.

She would. Emily was an intelligent woman. She'd listen to reason, put this behind her and get on with business.

Jake let out a breath he hadn't realized he'd been holding. Then he slung his coat over his arm and went outside, into the corridor. Emily wasn't there. He frowned, glanced at his watch, tapped his foot.

The door to the ladies room swung open.

"Emily," he said briskly...

It wasn't Emily. It was Crystal. When she saw Jake, she smiled.

"Hi, handsome. Waiting for me?"

"Uh, not exactly. Did you happen to see Emily Taylor in there?"

"Who? Oh, you mean that dowdy little... Your secretary?" Crystal batted her lashes. "Nope." She moved closer, her head tilted, her smile brilliant. Too brilliant, everything about her. The sprayed-to-stay hair, the bright red mouth, the endless eyelashes. "Is it really important? To find her, I mean?"

"Yes," Jake said, "it is."

Crystal's face fell but he didn't notice. Of course it was important, he thought, as he made his way through the crowded corridor. He had to find Emily so he could tell her that what had happened—what had almost happened—was a mistake.

On the other hand, he didn't have to tell her tonight. It might be best to let her down easy. Yeah, that was it. Take her home, see her in, maybe just kiss her again a few times, so she wouldn't be as upset when he said—

"Jake?"

Jake cocked his head. "Emily?"

"Jake. I'm over here."

Over where? There. Inside the jammed main room, he could just make out a hand waving in his direction.

"Excuse me," Jake said, and started towards that hand.

Emily, in the thick of the party? It amazed him, that she'd worked up enough courage to move ahead on her own. Well, that was an improvement. Getting her out among people had been a good idea. If only he could convince her to let him put his plan into motion. Introduce her to guys. Get her to go out on dates. It would be the right thing for her, especially if she harbored any silly ideas about him, now that they'd had that insane business in the elevator...

"Jake? Jake, here I am."

Jake almost skidded to a stop. "Emily?"

It was Emily, all right, but an Emily he'd never seen before. Her coat and jacket were gone. She'd taken all those loose curls and piled them high on her head, though several fell sexily around her face. Her blouse was closed but only as far down as the button that had started all the trouble because he could see that hint of white lace emphasizing the sweet curve of flesh rising above it.

Jake stared.

What had happened to her skirt? What had she done to it? A little while ago, it had hung somewhere between her calves and ankles. Now it hung just above her knees. It wasn't shapeless anymore, either; she'd cinched something around her waist. A belt. The belt from her coat? Yes, that had to be it. The belt, hugging her waist, holding up the skirt...

"Jake," she said pleasantly.

He blinked. She was smiling, smiling and hanging on to Thad Jennett's Armani-clad arm. And Thad was beaming down at her.

"We've been looking for you."

"Really," Jake said, when he could find his voice.

"Yes." She smiled at him, then at Thad, and just for a minute, Jake wanted to pound his fist into Jennett's slickly handsome face—but that would have been stupid because this was exactly what he'd hoped for, that Emily would meet some man to date.

"...waiting for you, when Thad came along, and..."

But not Jennett. Not without knowing more about him. Was he okay? Pete Archer was supposed to have been okay but look what had happened. The bastard had come on to Emily like an octopus.

"...that I had to wait until you..."

So, okay. Tomorrow, he'd do this the right way. He'd sit down, draw up a list of names. Guys he knew well enough to let Emily date them. It might take a while. He'd have to check their backgrounds, talk to people who knew them, talk to the guys themselves...

"...leave now, Jake, if you have no objection."

"No," Jake said. He smiled politely and reached for her

arm. "No, on the contrary. I was just thinking the same thing. Let's just get your coat and—"

"Oh, I didn't mean I was leaving with you," Emily said, with a brilliant smile. She looked up at Jennett, who smiled back at her. "Thad's asked me to supper."

"Supper?" Jake repeated, as if the concept was alien to him. "You, and Jennett?"

Jennett leaned forward, man to man. "Food's not up to par tonight, Jake, not up to par at all. Looks as if UBS had to cut corners, to make up for that extra two mill a year they've agreed to pay me on my new contract."

Jennett laughed. Emily smiled. Jake knotted his hands and jammed them into his trouser pockets.

"Thad? Would you get my coat, please?" Emily shifted closer to Jake as Jennett hurried off. "Jake, I want to be sure you understand that—that what happened in the elevator..." She licked her lips. "It was a mistake."

"Says who?" Jake snarled, as all his good intentions flew out the door.

"Oh, come on. You know it was."

"What I know is that going to supper with Jennett is a damn-fool idea!"

"It's an excellent idea." Emily touched his arm. "It was good of you to do what you'd said. Introduce me to a nice man, I mean."

"Jennett? That's your idea of a nice man?"

"Uh-huh. He's charming."

Jake's mouth thinned. "What he is," he said coldly, "is a one-man publicity machine. That smile's as phony as a three-dollar bill. I'll bet every tooth in his mouth is capped." He clasped her elbow and pulled her towards him. "And I don't know enough about Jennett to agree to a date."

Emily pulled free of Jake's hand. "Then it's a good thing he asked me out instead of you," she said sweetly.

"Dammit, Emily! You can't go out with anybody unless I say you—"

"Ready?"

Thad Jennett smiled at them both as he draped Emily's jacket over her shoulders.

"Completely ready," she said, with a cold look at Jake.

Jake thought about answering. He thought about punching out Jennett's lights. He even thought about slinging Emily over his shoulder and heading straight back to the elevator...

But he was a civilized man. And anyway, what did he care who his exec dated? Her life, and the men in it, were her business.

He got himself a drink, then scoured the room until he spotted Crystal.

"Crystal," he called, and when she turned and smiled, he held out his arms in welcome.

CHAPTER FIVE

JAKE stood at the window in his office, sipping a cup of what was supposed to be coffee.

It smelled right. It even looked right. But if coffee tasted like this, the world's tea-leaf growers would be billionaires.

He took another mouthful, shuddered and swallowed. This was what you got for relying on someone. It was Emily's job to make the coffee. Every morning, promptly at nine, she brought him a cup.

But she'd come to work too late to do it yesterday. Jake shot a scowling look at his watch. And she was going to be late today, too. There was no excuse this time. No snow. No tangled traffic. No subway trains running late. He'd had to make his own coffee and dammit, Emily obviously knew something about the coffeemaker he didn't because the stuff she made never tasted like this.

"Never," Jake growled, as he strode into his private bathroom and dumped the sludge down the sink.

The day was definitely not off to a good start.

Jake stomped back to his desk and sat down in his chair.

How could the day begin well, without a proper cup of coffee? Without the presence of his executive assistant? Without having a memory of an evening that should have been, to say the least, memorable?

"Damned right, it should have been," he mumbled.

Crystal was beautiful. Beautiful? She was spectacular. Yards of blond hair. Silky skin. A lush-looking mouth, a body that should have graced a centerfold. Oh, yes. Spectacular was the word. On a scale of one to ten, she was a twelve.

And what had he done? He'd taken her to supper, then home. He'd taken her to *her* home, and left her at her door with a chaste kiss on the cheek and a sort of promise he'd phone sometime soon.

Jake groaned, propped his elbows on his desk and buried his face in his hands.

In other words, the evening had been a disaster, and who was to blame for that? Not Crystal. Not him.

"Emily," Jake said, lifting his head and glaring at the door. Emily, that was who.

She'd ruined his evening, ruined his night, because he'd ended up so ticked off that he'd spent most of it tossing and turning instead of sleeping. She'd put him into a foul mood, and for what reason? All he'd tried to do was look after her. He'd taken her to a party, offered some helpful advice and had she appreciated it?

"No," he said, answering his own question.

In a city like this, most women would surely give anything for a man's concern. But his testy executive assistant hadn't just disregarded his advice, she'd tossed it in his face. She'd gone out on the town with a man who was wrong for her and now it was the next morning, and she was late.

Jake looked at the open door between the inner and outer office, then at his watch again.

Did she think he'd tolerate lateness, now that he'd promoted her and given her a raise? Maybe she thought that fooling around in the elevator had really meant something. It hadn't. She'd simply caught him by surprise with the lace thing. So what? Some men got turned on by high heels, some by silk. He just happened to like lace.

Not that he'd ever known it, until last night. Lace was, well, it was lace. Sexy, sure, but no more so than, well, than silk. Or satin. It was only that the lace had been so unexpected. Cotton, was what he'd have figured, if he'd figured anything at all...although even cotton would have done it, against Emily's soft, sweetly-scented skin. Against that smoothly curved breast that he'd barely tasted...

The outer door swung open. Emily stepped into the office,

covered from head to ankle in her usual layers of shapeless wool. But she wasn't shapeless. She was delicately curved, lushly female. He knew that, now.

Did Thad Jennett, that smarmy excuse for a human being, know it, too? Had Jennett kissed that sweet mouth, that delicate flesh? Had he stripped away Emily's coat, her jacket, her blouse…

"You're late," Jake snarled, and shot to his feet.

Emily shut the door, looked calmly at the clock on her desk, then at him. "And a cheerful good morning to you, too, Mr. McBride."

"There's nothing good about it." He folded his arms. "Well?"

"Well, what?"

"Well, aren't you going to explain why you're late?"

Emily went to her desk, put down her purse, pulled off her gloves and scarf, unbuttoned her coat. Carefully, she tucked her scarf and gloves into the pockets of the coat, hung the coat in the closet, then sat down and pulled off her boots. No heavy socks, Jake noticed. Just a quick, tantalizing flash of nylon-covered leg.

"I am not late. In fact," she said, with a nod at the clock, "I'm early." She smoothed down her skirt, pulled out her chair and sat. "Perhaps you've forgotten that I'm not due in until nine."

Jake's scowl deepened. The skirt was nubby wool, at least a hundred sizes too big, and hadn't he asked her to wear something else for tonight's cocktail party?

"I have forgotten nothing," he said coolly. "And I'd suggest *you* not forget that you have an obligation here."

"I beg your pardon?"

She didn't beg anything. He could tell, from the way she spoke, from the way she was looking at him. What had happened to business demeanor? Was this what came of a meaningless few fumbles in an elevator, or was it what happened after a meal with Thad Jennett?

"I asked you to wear something appropriate for this evening."

"This evening?"

"Yes. The party at Internet Resources. A business commitment which I see you've already forgotten."

"I didn't forget. I just…" Emily swallowed. "I can't go with you."

"Why not?"

"I—I just don't think it's a good idea."

"Perhaps I should remind you that you have an obligation—"

"You already did. And I'll continue to fulfill that obligation, each and every day."

Jake's eyes narrowed. "If that's a polite way of telling me that your nights are your own, I'd suggest you keep in mind that your days belong to me. You can carouse—"

"Carouse?"

"Exactly. You can carouse from dusk to dawn. You can light up the night, if that's your preference." He strode towards her, his expression chill, his hands on his hips. "Just don't expect to waltz into this office late."

"I told you, I am not late."

"My coffee is usually on my desk by nine."

"Only because I usually come in early."

"Well, then."

"Well, then, what?"

Well, then, Jake thought grimly, he was making a colossal ass of himself again. So what if she'd gone out with Jennett? So what if she didn't want to go out with him tonight? Go out? No. He'd intended to have her accompany him to a business function, that was all, and maybe she was right. Maybe it wasn't a good idea…

He clamped his lips together, marched into his office, shut his door and buried his nose in his work.

Ten minutes later, he shoved aside what he was doing,

pushed back his chair, went to the door and flung it open. Emily was typing away at her computer.

"You're right," he said.

She looked up. "Excuse me?"

"Your life is your own, to do with as you see fit."

"Am I supposed to say thank you?"

Jake's eyes glittered. "I'm trying to apologize, dammit."

Emily sighed. "I know. It's just… I'm not in the best of moods this morning."

"Yeah." He nodded, ran his hand through his hair. "Well, that makes two of us." He hesitated. Her life was her own, but there was nothing wrong in asking. After all, he was the one who'd introduced her to Jennett. "So, how'd things go?"

"Things?" she said brightly.

Too brightly, Jake thought, and cocked his head.

"Your date with Jennett. It, uh, it went well?"

She looked at him for a long moment. "Fine," she said, and smiled, but she wasn't fooling him. The smile was as phony as the perky voice.

"Emily?"

She shook her head, swiveled her chair so that her back was to him. "I have a lot to do, Jake. Those memos you left me yesterday…"

"Emily," he said again, and went to her. He put his hands on the back of the chair, turned it towards him. She dropped her head so he couldn't see her face and he squatted down beside her, gently cupped her chin in his hand and brought her eyes level with his. "Emily, what is it?"

Her shoulders lifted and fell. "Nothing. I told you, I'm just not in the best of moods this morning."

Jake sighed. "My fault. I'm sorry. I shouldn't have chewed your head off. Of course you weren't late. You never are."

"Yesterday," she said, and sniffed. "I was late yesterday."

"Yeah, well, so was half the city."

Was that a hint of dampness in her eyes?

"That cold I mentioned," she said, as if she'd read his thoughts. Jake nodded, dug in his trouser pocket, took out a folded white handkerchief and gave it to her.

"Blow," he said. He waited while she did, then cleared his throat. "It's just, well, when you didn't show up early, the way you usually do, I began to worry."

"About me?"

"Sure. I mean, I sort of feel like I'm responsible for introducing you to Jennett." He waited for her to say something. When she didn't, he cleared his throat again. "How'd it go? I mean, no octopus last night?"

Emily smiled. "Thad was a perfect gentleman."

Jake let out his breath. "Good. That's, ah, that's a relief to hear."

"But the date was a disaster."

"A disaster?" Jake frowned and rose to his feet. "How come?"

"It just was," she said, in a small voice.

"You didn't have a good time?"

"I was too nervous to have a good time."

"Nervous? About what?"

Emily sighed. "About everything. What to say. What to do. What to order, from the menu…"

"Where'd he take you for supper?"

"A little place on Third. It had a French name but Thad kept calling it a perfect bwaht, whatever that means."

Jake nodded. *"Chez Louis?"*

"That's it. But I've no idea what a 'bwaht' is."

"It's French, Em," he said gently. Oh, she was so innocent. Her mouth was trembling, and he thought about kissing it. Just to soothe it, of course, not for any other reason. "A *boite* is a box. Jennett meant the restaurant is like a little jewel box. A special sort of place." Indeed, it was. Jake knew it well. *Chez Louis* was one of midtown's most romantic,

most seductive restaurants. His jaw tightened. "He was trying to impress you."

"Oh, it was impressive, all right. Soft lights. Not a word
of English from the waiters or on the menu..." She looked
up at him. "I was never very good at languages. I took a lot
of science courses. I wanted to be an anthropologist. I
thought I did, anyway, until I decided I'd like to try my hand
at business..." Her words trailed away.

"Well," he said briskly, "dinner must have been nice."

Emily shrugged. Her eyes glittered again and she lifted his
handkerchief to her nose and blew.

"It wasn't?"

"I guess. But Thad ordered snails." She shuddered and
folded her hands in her lap, the handkerchief bunched in her
fist.

"Yeah." Jake smiled. "Well, some people love 'em. Me,
I've never been able to get past the idea that they leave a
trail of slime behind them when they... What?"

"He ordered them for me."

Jake's eyes narrowed. She'd let Jennett order her meal,
when she wouldn't even let *him* give her advice?

"I see," he said coldly.

"No. No, you don't. 'Why not let me order for both of
us?' Thad said, and I said, fine, because the menu was in
French and the only language I ever took was beginning
Spanish and..." She paused, took a deep breath. "He said
they were es cargo."

"Escargots," Jake said helpfully.

"Yes. Well, I'd heard the word. I mean, of course, I knew
it was some kind of French dish..."

"Of course." Was it possible his little sparrow regretted
her first flight? Jake squatted down beside her again and took
her hand. "But you didn't know exactly what."

"Not until the waiter put the plate in front of me." A
shudder ripped through her again. "Oh, when I saw those

slimy shells…" She sighed. "I couldn't eat them. And I felt so silly. I mean, I should have known he'd asked for snails."

"Lots of people wouldn't."

"I'm twenty-six years old," Emily said sternly. "I live in New York City. I'm going to meet lots of sophisticated people, now that I'm your exec. Don't you think it's time I could make my way through a restaurant menu, even if it's written in French?"

"It's probably a good idea, but it's not—"

"I made a fool of myself, is what I did, Jake!" Emily snatched back her hand, plucked some papers from her desk and got to her feet. Jake stood, too, and followed her slowly into his office. "I turned green at the sight of the snails, I nearly gagged over the drink he'd ordered for me…"

"What was it?"

"I don't know. Thad said it was an apéritif but it tasted more like cough medicine."

So much for Jennett's Let-Me-Thrill-You-With-My-Sophistication suaveness, Jake thought with satisfaction. That had obviously been the plan, but it had fallen flat on its cosmetically enhanced face.

"So," he said, trying to sound sympathetic, "it wasn't a memorable meal, huh?"

"I guess it depends on your definition of memorable." Emily blushed. "I felt like an idiot by the time it ended. You know, the poor little country mouse? That was me."

"Don't be silly. There's nothing wrong with not being familiar with menus deliberately written so you can't understand them, or with a drink that tastes like you ought to have somebody clamp your nose shut with one hand and pour it down your throat with the other."

He'd hoped for a smile. Instead, Emily dumped the papers on his desk and swung towards him, her expression taut.

"Don't patronize me, Jake. You said I'm going to have to attend business functions with you. Well, you won't think it's so amusing if I end up making an ass of myself when we're together.''

Jake sighed, eased a hip onto the edge of his desk and folded his arms.

"When I came to New York,'' he said, "I thought the height of fine dining consisted of a hot dog served with chili.''

Emily's lips twitched. "No, you didn't.''

"Yeah, I did. Back home, you ate a frank in a bun with mustard and, if you were lucky, sauerkraut. Then I came to the big city and discovered those pushcarts where you can order a hot dog smothered in mustard, ketchup, onions, relish, and chili.'' He grinned. "I can still remember standing on the corner, eating a frank with everything and thinking that was *haute cuisine*. Well, I'd have thought it if I'd known the phrase. As it was, I just figured I'd died and gone to heaven.''

Emily laughed. Damn, Jake thought, watching her, she had a wonderful laugh.

"Chili dogs are gourmet dining, huh?''

"Hey, this is New York.''

She laughed again. Had her laugh always been like this, so open and easy and infectious? Or had he just never noticed it before?

"Thank you, Jake. For making me feel better, I mean. All through supper, I just kept wanting the evening to end.''

"Ah.'' He cleared his throat. "Speaking of endings, how did it? End, I mean. What time did Jennett get you home?''

"I'm not sure. It wasn't late.''

"No?''

"No.'' Emily's smile faded. She took some papers from the desk and began leafing through them. "You left me a memo about that trip to San Diego. I have it here, somewhere...''

"Emily? What's the matter?''

"Nothing.''

"Come on, don't hand me that. Something's wrong."

Emily bit her lip, spun around and started towards the door. "I don't want to discuss it."

Jake could feel his muscles knot. "Well, I do," he said. He moved past her, shut the door, leaned back against it and folded his arms. His face was blank. "I thought you said he wasn't an octopus."

"He wasn't."

"So?"

"So…" Color suffused her face. "I don't think this is an appropriate topic of conversation for an employer and an employee."

Jake thought about taking Emily in his arms, kissing her until she clung to him, reminding her with his hands and mouth that what had gone on between them last night wasn't what either of them would have called "appropriate" just a few days ago, but that would only have taken things back to where they'd been in the elevator, and he wasn't going to let that happen.

He'd already reached that decision.

There wasn't a way in the world he was going to get involved with Emily…but he did have an obligation here.

"Remember what I said after your date with Archer? About feeling responsible?" He spoke calmly. Why wouldn't he? Just because her color was deepening and his imagination was running wild, why wouldn't he speak calmly? "I introduced you to him, too, and look what happened. Come on, Em. Tell me about last night."

Emily sighed. She put her hands behind her, placed them against the edge of Jake's desk and leaned back. The simple action thrust her breasts forward. Not that he could see them; she had on another of those big, bulky suit jackets. But he could imagine the way they were lifting, rising towards him. Towards his hands. His mouth…

Jake frowned and stood up straight.

"What did he do?" he demanded. "If that bastard got out of line—"

"We kissed," she blurted.

Jennett had kissed her. Jake curled his hands into fists until he could feel his fingernails biting into his palms. Well, so what? A kiss wasn't anything. And she had the right to kiss any man she liked. She had the right to sigh in a man's arms, open her lips to his, take his tongue into her mouth...

Jake cursed, grabbed his suit jacket from the back of his chair and made for the door. Emily flung herself in front of it.

"Jake? Where are you going?"

"To kill Jennett," he growled. "I don't know why you tried to protect him, why you said he wasn't all over you if he was, but—"

"He wasn't. He didn't. It was me. I...I kissed him!"

Jake felt everything inside him become numb. "You kissed him? But you just said—"

"I know what I said." Emily blushed. "This is so embarrassing!"

"Just tell me what happened, dammit." Jake tossed aside his jacket and dug his hands into her shoulders. "You kissed Jennett?"

"He kissed me first. At the door. On my cheek. And I— I thought, well, of course he's only going to want to kiss my cheek, after that dumb performance in the restaurant..."

"You wanted him to kiss your mouth," Jake said slowly. "You actually wanted that—that—" he drew a harsh breath "—that man to kiss your mouth?"

"You have to understand," Emily said, the words a breathless rush, but how could she make him understand when she still didn't? She'd told herself she'd wanted Thad to kiss her because he was handsome, and sexy; because he was only the second man who'd asked her out in years...

But the truth was far more complicated. It had to do with wanting, with hoping, that Jake's kisses hadn't turned her inside out because they'd been from Jake. That her response to him had been no different than it would be to any man, that it wasn't just his particular kisses that could make her feel as if time were standing still.

"Well?"

Emily looked up into Jake's face. He was waiting for her answer but she knew better than to tell him the things she'd been thinking. She might have been naïve about French menus and good-night kisses, but she knew better than to tell a man like Jake that his kisses robbed her of coherent thought and all but liquefied her bones.

"After the restaurant thing...I just—I felt like a ninny. I wanted to be cool and sophisticated. So, when I realized he was aiming for my cheek, I turned my head at the last second and—and he ended up kissing my mouth, instead." She swallowed hard. "And—and..."

"And?"

"And..." Her voice fell to a whisper. "Nothing."

"Nothing," Jake said. He knew he sounded like an idiot trapped in an echo chamber but what was a man supposed to say to a woman when she told him what it was like to kiss another man? "What do you mean, nothing?"

"No bells. No lights. No flutter in my... No flutter," she said, her face flaming. "It was pretty much like kissing a friend. I just didn't feel anything."

Jake wanted to shout hosannas. "Really," he said calmly.

"Really. And Thad knew it. He had to. I pulled back and I stuck out my hand and thanked him for supper and..." She gave a long, deep sigh. "And, that was it. There I was, kissing a man women dream about, and I bungled it."

"You didn't bungle it when I kissed you," Jake said softly.

"I know. And I don't understand it." Her eyes sought his. "A kiss is just a kiss, after all."

Jake smiled a little. "That's what an old song says, yeah."

Gently, he framed her face with his hands. His gaze fell to her lips, then rose again. "But it's not true."

"No?"

"No." His voice was calm. That, in itself, was remarkable because her embarrassed whispers were turning him on as much as if she were touching him. "Every man has a different technique."

"You think?"

"I know. Show me how you kissed him," Jake said, in a voice he barely recognized as his own.

"How I kissed Thad?" A warning bell sounded softly in Emily's ears. Don't, she told herself, oh, don't do this. But Jake's thumbs were moving over her skin; his eyes were blazing into hers. "Well..." Her heart began to race. "I told you. He bent down to kiss my cheek."

"Like this?" Jake said, tilting his face towards hers.

"Exactly. But at the last second, I sort of turned my head..."

"Turn it," he said, and his voice grew even deeper. "The way you did last night. Fine. Now, do the rest."

"Kiss you?"

"Yes. Kiss..."

She did. She tilted her face to his, brought her lips to his in a kiss so innocent, so gentle, that he felt his heart turn over.

"And Jennett didn't intensify the kiss?" he said, or thought he said. The blood was pounding in his ears; he was having trouble hearing anything but its heavy beat.

"He tried," Emily whispered.

"How? Did he put his arms around you, like this?"

Jake slipped his arms around her and drew her to him. Emily bit back a moan.

"No. I didn't give him the chance."

"Well, just in case he does, the next time, let's work on this a little, okay? Look up at me. That's it. Now, tilt your head, just a bit..." God. Oh, God, what was he doing? Why didn't he let go of her? Why didn't he write her a check for six months' salary, for a year's salary, give her a glowing letter of commendation and send her packing? "Now, part your lips, Em. Excellent. Stay like that. That's fine. Fine."

He bent his head and lightly, very lightly, feathered his mouth over hers. It was barely a kiss; it was a whisper of a kiss but the feel of her lips, the sweetness of them, instantly drove all the blood from his head straight into his groin.

"Like that?" she said shakily.

Yes. Like that. Exactly like that...

"No," Jake said. "Not quite. You have to open your mouth just a little bit more. Good girl. Now, relax. Lean into me..."

He groaned. He couldn't help it. The taste of her. Oh, the taste.

"How's that?" he said, his voice low, his body hard, his brain on the brink of combustion. "Better?"

"Better," Emily said, and sighed. "Much better."

Jake dipped his head again, settled his mouth over hers, slid the tip of his tongue between her lips and she made a sound, the sound a woman makes as she surrenders herself to a man, and he knew that if this went any further, if he didn't stop it now, he was going to take her. Strip away her clothes, all that foolish wool, carry her to the couch and take her...

"Jake?" she whispered, and she arched against him, kissed him, bit delicately into his bottom lip...and shattered his control, completely.

He sank down into the chair behind his desk with Emily in his lap. The clip fell from her hair as he tunneled his fingers into it; he felt her shudder and then her arms were tight around his neck, his hands were under her skirt, on her legs, her thighs; she was moaning into his ear and he was lost, he was lost, he was...

The phone rang.

"Jake," Emily gasped, but he shook his head, cupped her face, took her mouth in deep, hot kisses...

The phone rang, and rang, and finally Jake snarled, reached for it and jammed it against his ear.

"Hello," he said, "and this better be..."

The look on his face changed. He sat up straight, so suddenly that Emily almost fell off his lap. One glance at Jake's face and she scrambled to her feet.

"Glad to hear it," he said, after a minute. His voice was frigid, his eyes icy as he hit the mute button and held out the telephone. "It's for you."

"For...?"

"It's your boyfriend. Jennett." Jake's teeth glittered in a predatory smile. "You forgot to tell me why you can't make that party. You have another date with him this evening."

Emily's heart tumbled. "I didn't forget. Anyway, you didn't ask."

"No. No, I sure as hell didn't." He shot her another terrible smile. "Why would I? It's your life, Emily. Who you see is none of my business. Besides, I'm flattered."

"Flattered?"

"Sure. It's not every day I'm used as a stand-in for the real performance."

Emily turned pale. "You can't believe that!"

"Can't I?" Jake grabbed his jacket from the back of the chair. "Have fun tonight, babe. Just remember to give credit where credit is due, when you start turning ol' Thad on."

"It's Thad who'll deserve the credit," she hissed, "not you!" Angry tears blurred her vision. She turned her back on Jake as she put the phone to her ear. "Hi," she said brightly. "No, no problem. Uh-huh. Yes, I'd love to. I had fun, too. *The Gondola,* at six? Great, Thad. I'll see you then."

She heard the click as Thad hung up. Then she slammed the phone into its cradle and swung around, ready to do battle, but she was alone in the office.

Jake was gone.

CHAPTER SIX

EMILY looked up from her computer monitor and checked the clock.

It was almost five, time to stop work and get ready for her date with Thad.

She finished what she'd been typing, saved it to a disk, exited the program and shut off her computer.

Jake still hadn't returned to the office. She'd spoken to him once, in midafternoon, when he'd phoned to issue some crisp commands. The call had been brief and to the point, with no time wasted on pleasantries. He'd simply ticked off a list of things he wanted done, she'd said "Yes, Mr. McBride," or "No, Mr. McBride," and that was it.

Well, that was fine. It was the way it should be, the way it would be, from now on.

She'd had lots of time to think, after Jake had stormed off, and she'd reached a decision. Not the obvious one, she thought as she put away a file folder, not the first one that had popped into her head, because what was the point of quitting a perfectly good job when there was a far simpler solution?

All she had to do was turn back the clock.

Everything had been great until that fateful moment Jake had smiled and told her to stop calling him Mr. McBride. Such a simple thing, that easy descent into informality, but it had turned life upside down. Well, it was time to set things straight again.

When she saw Jake—when she saw Mr. McBride—to-morrow morning, she would tell him that they were going back to the old rules. She'd call him by his proper name, and he'd stay out of her personal life.

It went without saying that he'd never kiss her, or touch her, again.

Emily rose from her chair, took her purse and made her way to the ladies room. She switched on the light, went to the sink and briskly washed her hands and face.

She was glad she'd decided against leaving her job. It would be foolish to give up an excellent position with excellent pay for what were, basically, simple lapses in judgment. And Mr. McBride wouldn't fire her. He might be an easy mark for the Crystals and Brandies of this world but when it came to business, he was a tough, take-no-prisoners warrior. She did her job well, and he knew it. Hadn't he promoted her and given her a fat raise just a few days ago?

Emily turned off the water, reached for a towel and dried her hands and face.

Yes, he'd stormed out of the office in a rage but by now, he'd have calmed down enough to realize that the best thing he could do, the best thing they could both do, would be to go back to where they'd been. She'd be Emily, he'd be Mr. McBride, and the closest they'd ever come to anything of a personal nature would be on Friday evenings, when he'd smile politely and wish her a pleasant weekend.

Now to get ready for her date with Thad Jennett.

She leaned closer to the mirror and looked at herself critically. She saw wide-set chocolate-brown eyes, a nose that was okay set over a mouth that was nothing special. Average, she thought, just plain, average Emily.

She poked at her hair, neatly confined at the nape of her neck. It looked all right, she supposed; not sexy or glamorous the way the hairdos on all those women last night had looked, but at least the strands weren't curling this time. She hated those curls; they looked wild and uncontrolled and that wasn't her, that wasn't her, at all.

A touch of dark brown mascara might have been a good idea, if she'd known Thad had really meant it when he'd said he'd call. So would a better-looking outfit. Not that she had one. The only nonpractical things in her closet were the silk suit she'd mentioned to Jake—to Mr. McBride—and a bridesmaid's gown. She'd bought the suit for Serena's wedding and the gown for Angela's.

The gown was out of the question. It was long. It was frilly. Mostly, it was puce. The suit wouldn't have worked, either. It was an okay shade of pale apricot but she'd have frozen wearing it in weather like this, although none of those women last night had seemed terribly concerned about freezing in their excuses for dresses. That Crystal creature, especially, hadn't been concerned about frostbite but then, she'd probably figured some man would warm her.

Not some man.

Jake.

Had he? Had he taken Crystal out, after the party? Had he taken her home, put heat and color into her skin with his hands and mouth...

Emily glared at her reflection.

"Stop it," she said sharply.

What Jake did with women was none of her concern. She worked for him, that was all. Besides, she had Thad to think about now. There wasn't a woman alive who wouldn't sigh at her good fortune. Thad was handsome. He was interesting. He was famous enough so that women shot her envious little glances when they'd had supper last night...

But he wasn't Jake.

Emily frowned.

No. He wasn't Jake, and a good thing, too. Thad was a gentleman. He'd never hold her prisoner in a public elevator, kiss her until she was breathless, press her back against the wall and touch her until she was mindless with need...

Just thinking about it made her head swim.

Maybe some women liked that approach but she wasn't one of them. She'd never fantasized about being conquered. Why would she? An intelligent woman wanted time to think, to make informed, clearly planned choices. Thad was a man who'd give her that time. No sudden moves, with Thad. No hot, demanding kisses. Just reason, and a careful telegraphing of his intentions, the way it had been last night.

Thad wouldn't overwhelm her senses, as Jake did. He wouldn't drive all rational thought from her head.

Emily lifted her chin and eyed herself in the mirror again.

She was really looking forward to tonight. Too bad she hadn't told Thad she needed time to change. Well, it wasn't too late to do a little touch-up. She pulled off the hair clip, fluffed her hair. Then she opened her jacket, undid a couple of blouse buttons. She hiked up her skirt, too.

It had worked last night. She'd proven she could get attention from men. But she didn't want attention from men, she wanted it from Jake…

Emily blinked. She pulled her hair back into its clip, buttoned her blouse, closed the jacket and rolled down the waistband of her skirt.

"Take it or leave it, Thad Jennett," she said, "this is the real me."

La Gondola was *Chez Louis* by another name, or at least in another language.

It was small, intimate and dimly lit. And if the captain's greeting was anything to go by, she wasn't going to understand the menu here, either.

Still, only a coward would turn tail and run. So what if her comprehension of menu-Italian began with Chianti and ended with lasagna? So what if she was wearing more yards of fabric than all the other female diners were wearing, combined, or if each of them must have spent the whole afternoon on hair and makeup?

Looks, as her mother had often told her, weren't everything. She was bright, she was well-educated. She could carry on a conversation, get by with ordering Chianti and lasagna. As for the rest…wearing a designer dress and having a perfect face and an even more perfect mane of hair wasn't everything.

On the other hand, maybe it was.

And maybe turning tail and running was the better part of valor, but it was too late for that. Thad had already risen to his feet to greet her as the captain bowed her into the booth.

"EmilyDarling," he said, touching his cheek to hers as he clasped her hands, "you're here, at last."

Yes, she thought, she was here. And now that she was, she wished she weren't. Not because she was dressed wrong, or because she knew she'd never be able to read the menu, but because she was here with the wrong man.

Her name wasn't EmilyDarling, and she hated air-kisses, and Thad was wearing half a bottle too much of cologne. Jake never wore cologne; his scent was simply of soap and man, and she had the feeling that sharing chili dogs on a sidewalk with him really would be the best kind of fine dining...

She blinked.

"Yes," she said gaily, "I'm here, at last."

Thad drew her down beside him. "Did you have a long day, EmilyDarling?" He smiled. "You probably did. That boss of yours doesn't give you time to think. I'll bet he keeps you chained to the desk."

"He doesn't. I mean, that's not why I'm late. The crosstown bus—" She stopped, took a breath, and started again. "Sorry. You were joking, of course."

Thad smiled. "Your innocence is so charming. Well, I know just the way to relax you. Let's have a drink."

"Chianti," Emily said quickly.

Thad laughed. "Chianti," he said, and laughed again. "Don't be silly, EmilyDarling. *La Gondola* is known for its wine list."

A hovering waiter handed him what looked like the Manhattan telephone directory. Thad opened it, glanced through it, and ordered something unpronounceable. Moments later, a bottle was brought to the table and opened. Thad sniffed the cork, swished some wine in his mouth, and nodded.

"Excellent," he said briskly and the waiter poured the wine. Emily lifted her glass when Thad lifted his and took a sip of what surely had to be paint thinner. "Isn't that delightful, EmilyDarling?"

"Lovely," Emily replied, and tried not to cough.

"Well," Thad said briskly, "did you hear what happened at the Bishikoffs' the other night?"

Emily didn't know who the Bishikoffs were, much less what had happened. It seemed to involve a dining-room table, a frantic rodent, and a rather athletic Persian cat. She tried to make sense of the story, got as far as feeling sorry for the poor mouse, then gave up listening and just smiled and nodded and said "oh, really," whenever it seemed appropriate.

"Wonderful story," Thad said, chuckling at his own humor, "don't you think?"

"Wonderful," she agreed.

What am I doing here? she thought. And where was Jake, right now? Was he out with some woman? Was he looking across a table like this one, smiling into her eyes? Would he go home at the evening's end or would he spend the long night locked in another woman's embrace...

"Emily?" Thad said. "What would you like?"

Emily jerked her head up. There was a menu lying in front of her. It made the wine list look like a short story.

"Sorry," she said quickly, and opened the menu. If lasagna was listed in elegant gold script anywhere on those parchment pages, she didn't see it. Determinedly, she snapped the menu closed. "I'll have pasta."

"Excellent choice, EmilyDarling. How about trying the house special? You'll love it."

"I'm sure I will." Well, she would. She liked lasagna better but pasta had just popped into her head. How wrong could you go with spaghetti?

Thad started talking again, about the cat and mouse chase at the Bishikoffs'.

"Of course," he said, "we all had to pretend we hadn't noticed…"

Oh, of course not, Emily thought, with growing irritation. Jake wouldn't pretend, if something like that were taking place right under his nose. He'd laugh out loud, if it were funny. Or he'd have gone to the rescue of the hapless mouse, which somebody should have done, if she was getting parts of the story right.

"That poor mouse," she blurted.

Thad's eyebrows lifted. "Mice are just mice," he said gently. "Besides, what could anyone possibly do? It was the most undignified situation imaginable."

As if dignity mattered, at such a moment. Jake wouldn't think so. He wouldn't be trapped by convention…

And he would not eat what was being placed in front of her right now. Creamy tendrils of pasta, laced with a strange, midnight-black liquid. Emily shrank back in her seat.

"That's not mine," she said quickly. "I ordered—"

"Pasta alla Gondola," Thad said, leaning over her plate and inhaling. "Wonderful!" He looked up at the waiter. "I can never remember, Paolo. Is that ink from squid or octopus?"

Emily looked at her plate. "It must be octopus," she said faintly, staring at the tiny, eight-tentacled creatures she'd just noticed delicately peeking out from under the pasta, "unless those are made of rubber…"

Her stomach lurched. The fork dropped from her fingers and fell to the floor. "I can't—I just can't…"

Thad put a sympathetic hand on her knee. "Can't what, EmilyDarling?"

"Can't eat seafood," a familiar male voice said. "She's allergic to it. Isn't that right, Emily?"

Thad snatched his hand from Emily's leg. She jerked her head around…and saw Jake.

"Surprised to see me?"

Stunned, she thought. Stunned and delighted. God, he was so handsome. So big and gorgeous. And so smart! He'd saved her from her fate with one quick sentence.

"A little," she said carefully, and wondered if he could see the race of her pulse in her throat.

Jake sat down beside her in the booth. Thad shifted closer to the wall.

"It's a good thing I came along," Jake said, looking over Emily's head at Thad. "She's got this rare allergy to cephalopod mollusks"

Cephalopod what? Emily thought. "Oh, I certainly do!"

The booth was small; Jake was big and solid. Wonderfully solid, like an anchor in a storm, she thought as his thigh pressed against hers.

"Strange she didn't mention it, when I ordered dinner," Thad said coldly.

"Well, she was only recently diagnosed. Right, Em?"

"Oh, yes." The lie sailed from her lips with ease.

"It's terribly rare. Not many things contain cephalopod mollusks." Jake reached under the table and took her hand. Her fingers lifted, wove tightly into his. "Well," he said briskly, as he pushed her plate aside, "let's order you something you can eat. *'Pasta Amatriciana,'*" he told the waiter, who'd come hurrying to the table. "For the lady, and for me." He smiled at Emily. "No allergy problems with that, I promise."

Emily smiled back. Her heart was still bumping against her ribs. It was so wonderful to see Jake, to have him with her. Only because he'd dug her out of a hole, of course. Why else would she be this happy to see him?

"McBride?"

Thad's voice was icy. Jake smiled politely and looked at him. "Yes?"

"What are you doing here?"

"What are *you* doing here, Jennett?"

"Having dinner, but—"

"What a coincidence." Jake laid his hand, still joined with Emily's, on her thigh. "So am I. At least, I was about to when I noticed you guys. You don't mind if I join you, do you?"

"No," Emily said. She blushed. "I mean, if it's all right with you, Thad..."

Thad offered a taut smile. "Of course."

"Great," Jake said, and waved the waiter over again to order some wine.

The wine was delicious. So was the pasta. Emily dug into it with pleasure. Jake squeezed her hand and leaned closer.

"Good?"

"Yes." She smiled at him. "Thank you."

"No need to thank me," he said quietly. "I like my ink to stay in ballpoint pens, and things with too many arms belong in nightmares."

She laughed. Jake did, too.

"Did I miss something?" Thad asked stiffly.

"No," Emily said, with a guilty smile. It was too bad. Thad was a nice man. He just wasn't—he wasn't—

"So," Jake said, "did you hear what happened at the Bishikoffs' the other night?"

He told the story but it wasn't the same. He'd actually been there; he made the incident seem funny, even for the mouse.

"...grabbed the first thing I could find, which just happened to be the salad bowl, trapped the little guy in it, and took him away. The cat wasn't very happy. Neither was the lady seated to my right because the salad ended up in her lap, but..."

She was laughing by the time he finished. Thad wasn't. He sat beside her stiffly, his eyes fixed on his plate. Gradually, her laughter died. This was terrible. She'd agreed to dinner with one man but she was really spending the evening with another. Thad might be a pompous ass, but he deserved better than this.

"Thad?" she said softly.

"Yes?"

"I'm sorry."

Thad put down his fork. "I doubt it."

"But I am. I didn't expect Jake to—"

Thad swung towards her, eyes glittering. "I don't like playing stand-in for another man, Emily."

"Jake isn't anything to me!"

"I don't believe you."

"What would you like me to do? Sign an affidavit? Jake's just my employer. He isn't—"

"Sweetheart?"

Sweetheart? Emily looked at Jake. "What did you call me?"

"Ah." Jake gave her a crooked grin and lifted their entwined hands to the top of the table. "Sorry. I know how you are about keeping things private."

"Private?" Dammit, what was she doing, repeating his insane comments this way? She twisted her hand, tugged it free of his. "Really, Jake..."

"Really, Em." Jake's tone was soft, his smile pleasant but his eyes were dark, and narrowly focused on her face. "I think it's time I took you home."

"Are you crazy? You're not—"

"Now," Jake said coldly. "Right now." He looked past her, at Thad. "Unless you have a problem with that, Jennett?"

Thad didn't answer. His skin had taken on a pallor that showed through his out-of-season tan. Even the waiter, who'd been approaching with dessert menus, seemed frozen in place.

Emily flushed, dropped her napkin alongside her plate and rose to her feet. "It's been a lovely evening but Mr. McBride is right. I have to get home."

Jake rose, too, his actions as slow and deliberate as those of a panther. "The party's on me," he said. He pulled out his wallet and tossed a handful of bills on the table. Then he looped his hand under Emily's hair, around the nape of her neck. There was nothing casual in it; it was the touch of a possessive male, and a look at Thad, staring up at them, assured Emily that she wasn't the only one reading it that way.

"Em?" Jake said.

She thought of all the responses she could make, everything from calling Jake McBride a fool to slugging him, but making a scene would only make matters worse than they already were.

"Jake," she said calmly, and she let him drape her coat over her shoulders, put his hand in the small of her back and guide her away from the table, through the restaurant and out the door.

"Taxi," Jake snapped at the doorman.

"Not for me," Emily said. She wrenched free of his hand and swung towards him. "Just who do you think you are?" she demanded, her voice quivering with rage.

"Did you expect me to sit there and let Jennett paw you?"

"He was not 'pawing' me!"

"Come off it, Emily. Or maybe you didn't think I could see what was happening right under my nose."

"Nothing was happening, except maybe poor Thad was trying to figure out what you were doing, elbowing in on our date."

"Oh, give me a break! You were damned glad to see me."

"Only because you were better looking than that stuff on my plate!"

Jake glared at her. "You were glad to see me because I'm me, and you know it."

"My God, you're impossible! Six feet of outlandish ego."

"Six feet plus," Jake growled, and pulled her into his arms.

His mouth took hers with heat and hunger; his arms closed tightly around her. Emily made a little sound of indignation…and then she groaned, rose on her toes, flung her arms around Jake's neck and kissed him back.

"Sir? Uh, sir, your cab…"

Jake stepped back, kept one hand on Emily and dug in his pocket for a bill with the other. Then he marched Emily to the curb but she'd recovered her equilibrium by then.

"I'm not getting into a cab with you!"

Jake muttered something, opened the door and none too gently pushed her inside, got in after her and gave the driver her address. The taxi shot off down the street.

"Damn you, Jake!"

"You ought to thank me," Jake said coldly, "instead of cursing me."

"Thank you?" Her voice rose shrilly. "For what, huh? For letting Thad think that you and I—that I…"

"You don't give a damn what he thinks. Not unless you've lost all your common sense."

"Don't you get it? You made it look as if you—you had the right to—to—"

"I do have the right." Jake shot her a quick look. "We agreed on that, remember? I'm going to find men for you to date, vet them, see if they're a good match for you."

"We didn't agree. And even if we had, I don't want you involved in my private life. Not anymore."

"Forget the octopus on your plate," Jake growled. "If I hadn't turned up, you'd be dealing with a human octopus in another half hour."

"You are beyond belief, do you know that?" Emily folded her arms and glared at him. "If Thad wanted to give me a bad time, he'd have done it last night."

"I saw the way he was looking at you, as if his brand were stamped on your forehead."

"And how do you think you were looking at me? When you announced I was leaving with you, when you—when you touched me that way. When you—when you kissed me just now…" Emily looked away from him and stared out the window. "This whole thing has gone wrong. You're my boss, not my keeper."

"Yeah, well, maybe you need a keeper."

"You had no right to turn up at that restaurant."

"Coincidence," he said airily.

"Coincidence, my foot! I was on a date. A date, Jake! Do you understand the meaning of the word?"

Jake's mouth thinned. She was right. She'd been on a date and, no, he hadn't turned up by coincidence but what else could he have done? Emily had made him angry as hell earlier today, but that didn't change the facts. One, Jennett had a reputation. Two, Emily was naïve. And three—the biggest piece of the equation—three, it was his fault she was out with the guy.

He'd offered to introduce her to men but not men like Jennett. There were other guys out there, guys he'd be glad to introduce her to, and if he couldn't think of one of them, well, that was only because he hadn't had time to work on the problem.

Plus, Emily needed some pointers. She needed to know how to dress, how to look, how to handle herself in fast company, which was the kind she'd been with tonight. And he'd need time to teach her all that, every last bit of it…

The taxi jolted to a stop. Jake looked up. They were outside Emily's brownstone, and she was half out the door.

"Wait for me," he said to the cabby, and scrambled out after her.

"I do not wish you to see me in," she said coldly, as she marched up the steps.

"I don't care what you wish. I always see my…"

Jake frowned. Emily looked at him. "I'm not your anything, Jake, except your assistant."

His assistant. Yeah, she was. And that was fine; it was all he wanted her to be. Still, he'd made a deal and if there was one thing Jake McBride always did, it was keep his end of a bargain.

"You're right," he said.

Emily's brows lifted. "Well, well, well. Two apologies, in one day? Will miracles never cease?"

"I probably shouldn't have shown up at *La Gondola*."

"Probably? Try 'definitely.'"

Jake ran his hand through his hair. "It's just that I felt responsible."

"I don't need anybody feeling responsible for me. I'm a grown woman."

"Yeah. But I said I'd introduce you to guys, and—"

"Are we back to that?" Emily swung away, took her keys from her purse and jabbed one into the lock. "You are hereby absolved from all responsibility for introducing me to men. Okay?"

"Not okay." Jake caught her shoulders and turned her to face him. "It was a lousy idea," he said roughly. "Me saying I'd introduce you to guys. You're not ready for it. You were completely out of your league tonight."

"Thank you for that generous assessment."

"If Jennett sat any closer to you, you'd have been in his lap."

"Only because you crowded your way in."

"It's a good thing I did. He had a hand on your leg, when I got there."

"It wasn't on my leg. It was my knee, and it was only for a second. And it was a friendly gesture. He saw that I was upset when the waiter put that plate in front of me..."

"And why did that happen?"

"Because I couldn't read the menu," Emily said coldly, "and I was too proud to admit it. Any other questions?"

"Did it ever occur to you that Jennett should have told you what that dish was when you ordered it?"

"He just assumed—"

"He assumed you were as innocent as Little Red Riding

Hood, and that turned him on. Dammit, you don't need to learn about menus, you need to learn about men.'' Jake moved closer to her. ''I looked at you tonight—hell, I looked at you last night—and I felt…'' *What? What had he felt, watching her laugh at another man's jokes? Smile into another man's eyes?* ''I felt as if I'd tossed a sparrow into a room filled with hawks.'' His voice roughened. ''There are things you need to learn, Emily.''

Emily shuddered. The wind had shifted; it was blowing in over the East River, chill and forbidding. Surely, that was the reason she was shivering. It couldn't have had anything to do with Jake, with his proximity, with the sudden crazy desire she had to fling herself into his arms again.

''Is that the reason you kissed me?'' she said quietly.

''Yes. No. Dammit, Em—'' Jake drew a ragged breath. ''Look, I can help you. I can teach you about men. What they want from women. What they look for, what they expect. The male-female thing, the thing you don't seem to understand at all.''

Emily stared at Jake. He was right. He could teach her. He already had.

''Is that what you want to do?'' she said huskily. ''Teach me about the male-female thing?''

It seemed a long time before Jake answered. When he did, his voice sounded low and far away, even to his own ears.

''Yes. Yes, I do. And I promise you, Em, I'll teach you all you need to know.''

Everything came to a stop. The whispers of the city night, the moan of the wind, even the thump of Emily's heart as she lifted her eyes to Jake's face.

''Jake,'' she whispered. ''Jake, I don't think—''

No, he told himself wildly. No, she wasn't thinking. Neither was he. He felt as if he were standing in a dark tunnel, trying to find his way out only by feel.

He took a step back, jammed his hands into his coat pockets, knotted them into fists. ''It's too late to think,'' he said gruffly. "It's been a long day for both of us. We'll talk to-morrow morning. Ten o'clock."

"Ten..." Emily cleared her throat. "Ten o'clock?"

"Right."

He took another step, backed carefully down the stairs. Did she have to look at him like that? With her eyes so wide and dark, her lips parted? He could kiss her now. Hell, he could have her now. Take her in his arms, lead her upstairs, let it all happen, everything they'd both been fighting the past days or maybe the past year; he was beyond trying to figure it out.

But he wouldn't do it. What he'd do would be to teach her the things she needed to know about men. How to talk to them. How to see a pass and head it off. Nothing else, because Emily wasn't his kind of woman, or maybe he wasn't her kind of man. She was innocent and sweet; she had no idea how the game was played. She'd open her heart to a man, offer him everything and expect everything in return. Not little blue boxes from Tiffany's or long-stemmed hothouse roses but an intimacy that had nothing to do with what two people did together, in bed.

And that wasn't his thing.

He wanted her, yeah, but if he had her, what then? It would be over for him but not for her, and it wasn't his ego talking now, it was reality. Emily was a forever kind of woman but he wasn't a forever kind of guy. She'd look at him with those big eyes, she'd probably cry, and he'd feel like the worst kind of SOB as he walked away.

It was better to walk away now.

Jake took a deep breath.

It wouldn't kill him. Years from now, it might even make him feel pure and righteous to look back and remember that he'd done it. He'd walk away from temptation. Hell, he'd do more than that. He'd see to it Emily really did meet a man, not just one to date but one who cared about her. A guy she could be happy with.

It was the right thing to do.

"Ten o'clock," Jake said gruffly.

Then he did the hardest thing he'd ever done in his life. He turned his back on Emily, got into the waiting taxi, and rode off into the night.

CHAPTER SEVEN

AT NINE the next morning, the clock radio beside Emily's bed shattered the silence with an earsplitting blast of guitar-twanging, drum-thumping, cymbal-crashing acid rock.

She shot up against the pillows, threw out her hand, knocked over a book, an empty cocoa mug and a box of tissues as she groped for the Off button.

The music stopped. Her heart pounded on. She waited until it slowed. Then she swung her feet to the floor and blinked at the radio.

She kept it set to a classical music station. Promptly at six each morning, Monday through Friday, the radio awakened her to the soothing strains of Debussy or Bach. Once in a very great while, she opened her eyes to something as modern and daring as Stravinsky.

But not rock. Never rock. It was too loud, too boisterous, too obvious, too everything. She'd always thought so. So, why would the radio be playing rock music this morning? For that matter, why would it go off at all, on a Saturday? And if it did, why would it go off at...

Nine?

"Nine," Emily gasped, and hurtled from the bed.

She remembered, now. Remembered it all. How she'd paced the floor last night, instead of sleeping. How she'd tossed and turned, once she'd finally fallen into bed. How she'd felt herself tumbling into the kind of exhausted sleep she feared would leave her feeling groggy, and how she'd reached out, fumbling in the dark, to reset the clock from six to seven so she'd have one more hour of sleep but would still awaken early enough to phone Jake and tell him there

109

wasn't a way in the world she'd see him at ten or any hour on a Saturday, in this lifetime.

Emily groaned.

There were two morals to that sad little tale. The first was never to try and set a clock radio in the dark. The second was never, ever, to let Jake McBride get the last word.

Nine o'clock! Hurriedly, she grabbed the phone and dialed his number.

"Come on," she whispered, "pick up, pick up, pick…"

"Hi," Jake said cheerfully.

Thank God!

"Jake?" Emily cleared her throat. "Jake," she said briskly, "I'm glad I—"

"This is Jake McBride. Sorry, but I can't take your call right now. Just leave your name, a brief message, and—"

Emily slammed the phone down. She scrubbed her hands over her face, ran them through her hair. She could feel curls springing up all over her head. What to do, what to do?

Calm down, an inner voice said.

But how could she calm down, when it was nine-fifteen and Jake was due here at ten? Okay. Okay, forget about calming down. She'd just concentrate on getting ready. Showering. Dressing. Doing something with her horrible hair, which seemed to know that there was snow forecast for later today. Then she'd put up coffee, straighten the house…

She sagged against the nightstand.

Forget about straightening the house. Forget about coffee. Just shower and get dressed, because the last thing she wanted was for Jake to ring her doorbell while she was standing here in her flannel pajamas.

No. He wouldn't be able to ring the doorbell. He'd have to press the downstairs buzzer. Then she'd have to press the Talk button. She'd say, "Who is it?" And he'd say, "Jake. Buzz me in," and she'd say, "Sorry, but I've changed my mind, Jake. I'll see you Monday morning, at the office…"

Buzzzz.

Emily spun around and stared into the living room. That was either the downstairs buzzer or an angry hornet had gotten into the house. It couldn't be a hornet, not in the winter. And it couldn't be the buzzer. Jake was coming at ten, and it wasn't even half past...

Buzzzz.

Then again, it didn't have to be Jake. It could be someone else. The super, calling to tell her when the painters would be coming. Or old Mrs. Levy, from apartment 3G, who forgot her keys half the time she went out and then just pressed buzzers at random until somebody buzzed back and let her in...

Buzzzz, buzzzz, buzzzz.

Whoever it was, was getting impatient. Her canary, its cage still covered for the night, gave a wistful chirp from the kitchen in response. Emily hurried to the intercom in the wall beside the front door.

"Yes?"

"It's Jake."

She groaned, closed her eyes, leaned her forehead against the wall. Actually, she felt like banging it against the wall but Jake might think she was trying to tap out a message.

"Emily?"

"Yes, Jake. I heard you. What are you doing here? It's not ten yet."

"Yeah, well, I got an early start."

"I'm not..." She looked down at her old pajamas, at her bare feet. "I'm not ready."

"No problem. I brought the paper. I'll just read it and wait."

"Fine. I mean, not fine. I mean, I've changed my..." Emily sputtered to a halt. Okay. Jake was here. In that case, she'd do the right thing. Get dressed, go downstairs, tell him her decision in person. "Look, just sit on the stoop and read the paper. I'll be down in twenty—"

"Are you nuts? It's zero degrees out here, Emily."

"Five minutes, then. That's all it'll take me to get ready."

"What's that, dear?"

"And don't 'dear' me!"

"I was talking with a charming lady name of... What's your name, sweetheart? Ah. Her name is Mrs. Levy. She says she forgot her keys and she's getting awfully cold, standing out here while you refuse to buzz her in."

Emily narrowed her eyes. "I hate you, Jake McBride," she said dispassionately, and pressed the buzzer. She thought about combing her hair, putting on her slippers, washing her face...

Instead, she flung open the door, folded her arms, and waited.

Jake bounded up the stairs a moment later. Her heart bounded, too. She'd never seen him dressed in anything but a suit. Today he wore scuffed leather boots, faded jeans and a scarred black leather jacket. Not that it mattered. He was an unwelcome sight...

But a magnificent one. Her heart leaped like a jackhammer when he smiled.

"Good morning, Emily."

"There's nothing good about it."

Jake went from a smile to a grin. "That's what I love," he said, "being greeted by someone who's cheerful, first thing in the morning."

What he hadn't expected to be greeted by was a barefoot, sleep-tousled Emily in a pair of flannel pajamas. He was a man who'd seen more than his fair share of slinky black nightgowns, negligees and spike-heeled sandals. How could a pair of bare feet and oversized flannel pj's be a turn-on? Not too oversized, though. He could see the rounded outline of Emily's breasts beneath the softly faded fabric, even see the thrust of her nipples...

Jake frowned. "We had an appointment," he said gruffly. "You look as if you just got out of bed."

"Our appointment was for ten o'clock. Besides, I changed my mind."

"Yeah, I figured you would."

Emily spun around as he brushed past her. "Where are you going?"

"I'm looking for the kitchen. You do have one, don't you?"

"Yes, but—"

Jake dumped the *Times* and a white paper sack on the kitchen table. "Two containers of coffee, two bagels with cream cheese, and two jelly doughnuts. My penance, for showing up early." He folded his arms. "I figured I'd better, or you'd chicken out."

"I am not, as you so elegantly put it, 'chickening out.' And I'm not interested in starting my day with a carbohydrate high."

"No problem. I'll eat the doughnuts by myself." Jake looked around the room. He'd have looked anywhere, if it meant not looking at Emily. Her hair was a mass of silky curls; her mouth was pink. What would she taste like, without even a touch of lipstick? What would she feel like, in his arms? Desperate for diversion, he jerked his chin in the direction of Horace's cage. "Is this the bird you told me about?"

"Yes. That's Horace. And he doesn't like strangers."

"Horace, huh?" He whisked the cover off the cage. "Named for the Roman poet?"

"Why—why yes. How did you—"

"Hello, Horace." Jake raised an eyebrow. "Does the lady underestimate you as often as she underestimates me?"

Horace sent up a trilling song. Emily glared at him, then at Jake, and gave up.

"Enjoy your breakfast," she said coldly, and started from the room. Jake snagged her wrist.

"I brought breakfast for two."

"And I told you, I don't like—"

"I heard you. Well, at least have the coffee, while it's hot. Oh, come on. It's not as if I've never seen the early-morning you."

Damn the man. He was making her blush. "You've seen me in the office," she said stiffly.

He smiled. Slowly, as if he had all the time in the world, he looked her over from the top of her head to the tips of her toes, then back up again.

"Right," he said softly. "In the office. And I have to tell you, this is a big improvement."

Emily's blush deepened. "I hardly think so."

"Well, that's where we differ. I find flannel and a wild mane of hair a lot sexier than a clip at the nape of your neck and an oversized tweed suit."

"I do not dress to look sexy, Mr. McBride."

"No." Jake's smile tilted as his eyes locked on hers. "You most certainly don't, Miss Taylor. But you should. That's going to be at the top of today's agenda. Lesson one—How To Dress For A Man."

"There is no agenda, today or any day. No lessons. I phoned to tell you that, but you'd already left your... What are you doing?"

It was a dumb question. What he was doing was curling his hand around the back of her neck, threading his fingers into her hair, moving closer to her, so close that she could smell the cold and the promise of snow on his skin.

"Jake." Emily cleared her throat. "Didn't you hear me? I've decided against your—your proposal. If I meet men, I'll do it on my own, and my own way. I don't want you to—"

Jake bent his head, brushed his lips gently over hers. Emily caught her breath. The touch of his mouth was light, so light she might have imagined it, but oh, she hadn't. She'd felt the kiss, the electricity, straight down to her toes.

"Jake." Her voice was shaky. "Please..."

"Please, what?"

His arms went around her. One hand slid under her pajama top and pressed gently against her naked back.

"Stop," she said, or tried to say, but Jake was tugging her closer, smoothing his hand up and down her spine.

"I'm just demonstrating," he whispered, his mouth soft against her ear. "Think of it as lesson one. How To Say Good Morning."

"You said…" Emily bit back a moan. "You said lesson one would be—would be How To Dress For A…"

Oh. Oh, he had to stop doing that. He had to let her go. Or maybe she had to let him go because somehow, her hands had stolen up his chest; her fingers had danced into his hair; she was drawing his head down to hers, his mouth to hers…

Jake clasped her shoulders and stepped back.

"Coffee," he said hoarsely. "I'll have coffee while you get some clothes on."

Emily swayed unsteadily. "Yes. Good. You have coffee while I…"

She turned, fled for the safety of the bedroom. Jake watched her go, told himself not to be an ass, not to go after her…

The door swung shut. He swallowed hard, felt for a chair, and sank into it.

So much for all his good intentions. He'd spent the night telling himself he'd done the right thing, when he'd walked away from Emily. That he was wrong for her. That she was wrong for him. He'd even gone through his address book, searching for the names of guys she might like. He had the list right here, in his jacket pocket.

And then he'd seen Emily standing in the doorway wearing an outfit that not even Marilyn Monroe in her heyday could have turned into something sexy, with her hair uncombed and her eyes a little puffy from sleep, and he'd had to work at not sweeping her into his arms and carrying her to bed.

Jake popped the lid off one of the cardboard containers,

dumped in half a dozen packets of sugar, stirred the resultant mess and gulped a mouthful. Caffeine, a sugar high and whatever the cardboard residue might add to the mix was just what he needed. Either that, or a cold shower.

He groaned, downed the rest of his coffee, grabbed one of the bagels and bit into it. He'd bought plain bagels, not the garlic ones that were his favorites. Big mistake. All those old movies on late night TV about werewolves and vampires... Wasn't it garlic that was supposed to keep them away?

Maybe it did the same thing when it came to keeping a man away from a woman he knew he shouldn't want.

Jake gave a soft, unhappy laugh. Where was a garlic neck-lace, when you need one? And how in hell was he going to make it through the day?

He paced, paced some more. He could hear the shower running. Not a cold one. A warm one. And Emily was in that shower. She was naked, waiting for him...

Jake grabbed the paper, buried his face in it and went through the motions of reading, but he'd given up the pre-tence by the time Emily entered the kitchen again. He was standing at the window, his back to her, and her breath caught at the sight of him.

He'd taken off his leather jacket; he was wearing a blue chambray shirt with the sleeves rolled midway up his mus-cled forearms. His hands were tucked into the back pockets of his jeans. His shoulders were broad, his waist and hips narrow, his legs long and slightly spread. It was the posture of a man who was self-assured and just a little dangerous.

Emily's throat tightened. She'd thought about Jake, while she was showering. There was no lock on her bedroom door, or on the adjoining bathroom. And she'd shut her eyes, while the water beat down, and imagined the shower door opening and Jake, a naked Jake, stepping into the shower with her. She'd imagined the strength of his arms, the feel of his mouth...

She must have made a sound because suddenly Jake turned towards her.

"Ready?"

She didn't trust herself to speak, not right away. To kill time, she went to the hall closet and got her jacket.

"Yes," she said, when it was safe to face him again. "I'm ready. What's on the agenda? New clothes? New hairdo? I made up my mind, Jake. I'm yours to command."

Jake felt his jaw knot so tightly it hurt. She wasn't. She was his for today, and only so he could ready her for another man.

What the hell kind of idiocy was that?

A sane idiocy, he told himself, without even wincing at the contradiction. He reached for his jacket, shrugged it on, and followed Emily out the door.

Snow did funny things to Manhattan.

On weekdays it snarled traffic, slowed buses and subway trains, piled up along the curbs and turned rapidly into slush.

It could do all those same things on a weekend...but nobody seemed to notice. The lacy white flakes touched the city with magic. People had even been known to smile at each other as they hurried along the streets.

Not Jake.

He didn't feel a bit like smiling.

He was seated in a leather and chrome chair built for contortionists in the waiting area of a place called *THE BEAUTY SPOT*. Mirrors surrounded him; music assaulted his ears. It came from every possible direction, some stuff he couldn't imagine anybody could possibly enjoy especially if their mood, like his, kept alternating between mean and downright nasty.

This was their third, and last, stop of the day.

He'd sat through a session in Saks, while a gushing saleswoman brought out suits and dresses, pants and blouses and sweaters, shoes and handbags and who knew what else, for Emily to try on...

Try on, for his approval.

At first, he'd liked the idea.

He had a pretty solid notion of how Emily ought to look. He knew she should wear soft colors and earth tones, that she had legs that deserved showcasing, that she had a body that deserved gently clinging cashmeres and silks. So, for a while, it had been a kick to sit in a velvet chair that was half a size too small for comfort, arms folded, head cocked, and say "No," "Yes," "Great," each time Emily stepped out of the fitting room.

"Your lady is so lovely," the saleswoman kept saying, and all at once, maybe the sixth time she said it, Jake had stopped grinning like an idiot and saying yes, yes, she was, because it had suddenly hit him that Emily wasn't his lady. She was his executive assistant and now she was his development project, and what he was "developing" her for was another man.

How come he'd forgotten that, somewhere between leaving her apartment and sitting through a fashion show?

Things had gone downhill from there.

He must have looked it, too. The saleswoman had stopped gushing, Emily had started giving him quick little glances, and when they'd finally left Saks with her wearing a cashmere dress in softest rose, a pair of high-heeled black leather boots and a belted black coat that looked soft as velvet, she'd said that if he wanted to call it a day, that was fine.

What he'd wanted was to call her beautiful, as she stood there with her face turned up to his—a face now heightened with artful applications of soft black mascara and lip gloss that matched the rose dress, after a stop at the cosmetics counter.

Instead, he'd taken an armful of elegant boxes from her, scowled and said that he'd made a deal and he was going through with it.

Which was how come he was sitting here, in *THE BEAUTY SPOT,* surrounded by glassy images of himself, images that pretty much showed a man coping with a growing frustration that made absolutely no sense at all. What was there to be frustrated about? This had been his idea, this makeover. And it was going well. Emily looked beautiful and, until he'd turned into a snarling beast at Saks, she'd been happy.

Well, that was her problem. She wanted to be happy because he was grooming her for another guy, let her. He didn't have to do anything except sit here with his arms folded, his back straight, his feet crossed at the ankles.

Jake glowered at himself. Half a dozen Jakes glowered back, all of them looking like police bulletins for the criminally insane. It didn't help that he hadn't bothered shaving this morning and he had a dark stubble on his cheeks and jaw. All in all, he might as well have been wearing a sign that said Keep Away. And people were. The place was crowded but the chairs on either side of him stayed empty and a good thing, too, because the last thing he wanted was to end up with some damned fool trying to engage him in polite conversation.

He was having a rotten time, and he didn't much care who knew it.

Emily, on the other hand, was back to enjoying herself.

Jake's eyes narrowed.

Eric, who was cutting her hair, was having a blast, too. Jake could see him from here, standing over Emily, smiling and laughing as he wielded a pair of scissors and a comb. She was laughing, too.

Jake's mouth turned down.

What the hell was there to laugh about?

The SOB better not be taking off too much of all that sexy hair. "Just trim it," Jake had warned, when he'd handed Emily over.

"Trust me, Jake," Eric had said.

Well, yeah. That was the reason he'd brought Emily here, wasn't it? He and Eric worked out at the same gym. They'd had some beers together. And Eric owned one of the trendiest styling salons in the city.

He was also straight, Jake thought grimly. And it was just possible some women might be turned on by his Viking good looks.

How come he hadn't considered those things before he'd brought Emily here and put her in Eric's hands? How come it hadn't occurred to him that Eric wouldn't just cut her hair, he'd also see how beautiful she was, how much fun; he'd see that she wasn't anything like the other women who crowded *THE BEAUTY SPOT,* that she was...

"Hi."

Jake lifted his glowering face. Emily stood before him. Eric was there, too, but at first all Jake could see was Emily. Emily, with her hair loose, with her curls set free, shiny and dark as coffee as they tumbled around her face.

"Well?" She smiled nervously. "What do you think?"

What did he think? Jake rose from the chair. What he thought was that he wanted to reach out and touch one of those curls, feel the silken whisper of it as he brought it to his lips....

"Not bad," he said calmly.

Emily's smile drooped. Good, Jake thought savagely. Had she really imagined he'd tell her she looked—she looked—

"That's typical," Eric said. He grinned, looped an arm lightly around Emily's shoulders and gave her a quick hug. "Last time I beat him at racquetball, he said the same thing."

Jake looked at Eric. "You got it wrong, buddy," he said quietly. "I beat you. And since when do stylists get so cozy with their clients?"

Emily flushed. Eric raised his eyebrows. Jake felt like an idiot.

"Oh, hell," he muttered, "man, I'm sorry. That was a stupid thing to say. I just—"

Eric let go of Emily and smiled. "No harm done, Jake. I'd probably have the ol' green-eyed monster on my back, too, if this were my lady."

"But I'm not," Emily said quickly. "I'm not—"

"See you," Jake said. He clasped Emily's arm and hustled her out of the salon.

"You shouldn't have done that," she hissed. "Now he thinks you and I—he thinks we're—"

"Did he ask for your phone number?"

"No!" Emily wrenched free of Jake's hand and glared at him. "But what if he had?"

What, indeed? Jake dug his hands deep into the pockets of his jacket. "Don't worry about it," he said coldly. "I'll set him straight when I see him next time. Once he's sure you and I aren't involved, he'll ask you out."

"I don't want him to ask me out! That's not what this is about."

"Sure it is. What else am I doing this for, if not to make guys interested in you?"

"I don't like your attitude!"

"You don't have to like it," Jake snarled. "Just do as you're told so we can get through the day."

"You know what?" Emily blew a curl off her forehead. "I've changed my mind. I don't want to get through the day. I don't want you in my face. In fact, I'm going home."

She swung away. Jake reached out, caught her arm and spun her towards him.

"You'll go home when I say you can go home."

"I know this may come as a shock, Mr. McBride, but I don't have to take orders from you."

"Yeah, you do. You're my exec, remember?"

"Five days a week. Even Scrooge gave Bob Cratchit weekends off."

"So, you're telling me you won't work overtime?"

Emily blinked. "What kind of question is that?"

"What do you think today is, if not overtime?"

"Huh?"

Huh, was right. Think fast, Jake told himself, go on, find a way to dig yourself out of the mess you're in.

"I have to drive to Connecticut, to, ah, to check on some property." Well, he thought, it could have been the truth. He had been planning to head north; he just hadn't thought about doing it today.

Emily frowned. "So?"

"So, I need you to come with me."

"To Connecticut?"

"Isn't that what I just said? Yes. To Connecticut."

"I don't understand. What does property in Connecticut have to do with me?"

"I want to see if you have a feel for this sort of thing."

"*What* sort of thing?" Emily shook her head. "I'm not following you at all."

Jake took her arm again. He led her up the street, around the corner, to where he'd parked his Corvette, unlocked the door and closed it after her. It took a couple of minutes, just the time he needed for it all to come together.

"There are times I invest in land," he said briskly, as he dumped the packages in the car and got behind the wheel. "You know that."

"Actually, I didn't. I know you have a weekend place in Connecticut, but—"

"Exactly." He checked for traffic, then pulled away from the curb. "The two acres next to mine just came on the market. I have to decide whether or not to buy them."

True again, he thought. Yes, it made more and more sense that she spend the rest of the day with him.

"And?" Emily said, sounding even more puzzled.

"And, I want your opinion. As my executive assistant."

He glanced over at her. She was looking at him as if he'd lost his mind and maybe he had. But his mouth was already working, even though his brain seemed to be shutting down.

"I have the data. Prices in the area. Tax info. Resale, all

of that." Jake cleared his throat. "Of course," he said politely, "if you think you'd be in over your head—"

"I'm perfectly capable of understanding the data," Emily said coolly. "I just don't understand why you didn't mention this before."

"I didn't think of it."

That was true enough, too. Suddenly, he knew how crazy he had to sound. And this *was* crazy. Why would he want to take Emily to Connecticut? He'd said he'd spend the day getting her new clothes, a new hairdo, new makeup. Well, he'd done it. She wanted to go home and it was time to let her do just that, then head to his place, check his address book, figure out who he felt like seeing tonight…except he didn't feel like seeing anybody, except Emily.

McBride, what are you doing?

"Listen," he said quickly, "if you don't want to do this… If you'd rather I took you home…"

He fell silent. The seconds ticked away and then Emily cleared her throat. "No," she said softly, "no, don't take me home. Take me with you, to—to Connecticut."

Suddenly, Jake felt as if the car were filled with electricity. He looked at Emily. She was sitting very still, her hands folded in her lap.

"Okay," he said gruffly, and he took the 'Vette onto the highway that led out of the city, then onto the Hutchinson River Parkway, headed towards northwestern Connecticut. He was silent. Emily was, too. He glanced at her once in a while, as they left the city behind and entered the wooded hills of southern New England. She sat as she'd been sitting, hands folded, staring straight ahead.

What was she thinking?

The roads were fairly empty. The snow, falling more and more heavily, was keeping people home. Hell, home was where he ought to be. There was no sense to this. He'd get Emily to his house and then what? Show her the stuff about taxes and prices in Litchfield County? What for? The truth was that he didn't need her opinion. He'd already decided to buy the land, not as an investment but because he loved the house, loved the hill it stood on, the forest that surrounded it.

Jake cursed, swung the wheel hard to the right and pulled onto the shoulder of the highway. He stared straight ahead while he gripped the steering wheel hard. His knuckles turned white.

"This is crazy," he said gruffly. "I'll take you back."

"Jake?"

"Yes?"

"Jake, look at me."

He did. For the first time in hours, he looked straight at her. His heart turned over. She was so beautiful. So beautiful...

"Is this really about property that's for sale?" she said softly.

Her eyes lifted to his, and what he saw in their chocolate depths stole his breath away.

"Hell, no," he whispered. Quickly, he undid his seat belt, undid hers, and reached for her. She came into his arms with a little sob, turned her face up to his and met his hard, hungry kiss with an eagerness that almost undid him.

"Emily," he whispered, "come with me. Let me teach you the things that really matter."

She put her hands in his hair and dragged his mouth down to hers.

"Yes," she said, against his lips, "oh, Jake, yes."

CHAPTER EIGHT

THE country road wound through the trees like a black ribbon, glittering wetly in the headlights of Jake's Corvette.

The windshield wipers beat a steady, swift pattern as they tried to keep up with the falling snow.

Emily was surprised the road was passable at all. She'd said as much, to Jake.

"It'll be clear," he'd said tersely. "The plows are always out early, especially in a storm like this."

The brief exchange had taken place almost an hour ago. Jake hadn't spoken a word since then.

Emily couldn't blame him. Ever since he'd pulled away after kissing her, she'd sat stiffly in her seat, her fingers almost painfully knotted together in her lap. Jake had to be thinking exactly what she was thinking, that the two of them had made an awful mistake.

Lights glinted ahead.

"Litchfield," Jake said.

The sound of his voice startled her. She looked over at him, nodded, searched desperately for something to say in reply as they drove through the town, which lay quiet under its heavy white mantle of snow.

"It's—it's beautiful."

"Yeah."

"It looks familiar. I know that's impossible. I mean, I've never been to this part of Connecticut before, but..."

"You've probably seen pictures of it on postcards. Typical New England scene, etcetera, etcetera."

It was a short, almost abrupt answer, delivered in a gruff tone. So much for conversation, Emily thought, and looked straight ahead again.

There was no question about it. Jake was definitely sorry he'd asked her to come with him. She could hear it in his silence, see it in his stern profile, in the way his hands gripped the steering wheel. He was as tense as an overwound spring.

Well, so was she. Jake's regrets couldn't be any greater than hers.

Emily clenched her hands together in her lap.

What insanity had made her say yes to his proposal? Why had she said she wanted him to teach her all those things she didn't know? It wasn't as if she'd misunderstood him. He was talking about things that happened in bed.

And she'd agreed. She hadn't even been subtle about it. She'd made it clear sleeping with him was precisely what she wanted but she shouldn't have. She wasn't cut out for a quick tumble in a man's bed.

In Jake's bed.

Yes, she wanted to know what sex was like. There was something pathetic about reaching this age and knowing only what you'd been taught in Sex Ed, back in high school, or what you'd picked up, over the years, from other women's comments. Her sisters, especially, made lots of references to sex. Barbed references, that suggested the whole thing wasn't half as terrific as it was cracked up to be.

Emily wanted to know for herself. She'd thought she did, anyway.

Now, with all this time to consider what came next, she wasn't so sure.

Was she really supposed to have sex with Jake tonight, go home tomorrow, then show up at work on Monday as if nothing had happened? She had no foolish illusions; this wasn't an affair she was entering into with him. He'd made that clear. This was part of her transformation from wall-flower to woman.

Next week, maybe even sooner, she'd be ordering flowers for his latest conquest, making his dinner reservations, behaving politely when some new candidate for McBride's Playmate of the Month telephoned.

"May I speak to Jake, please?" they always said, in breathy voices that made her think of satin sheets and chilled champagne.

Or they'd show up at the office and she'd be expected to smile politely when he slid his arm around a slender waist and left for the weekend with some oversexed, overdressed, overeverythinged female...

Oh, God!

Emily swung towards Jake. "Stop the car!"

He responded instantly and stood on the brakes. The Corvette gave a sickening lurch. Emily gave a thin scream as Jake fought for control of the car as it slid crazily across the slick blacktop and spun in a drunken circle.

When the car finally came to a stop, it was pointed towards the forest, its headlights burrowing a cavern of light into the darkness. The engine coughed and died. In the sudden silence, Emily could hear the roar of the wind, the rasp of Jake's breath and the thump-thump of her own heart.

"Holy hell!" Jake reached for her hand and squeezed it hard enough so she felt the imprint of his fingers. "Em? Are you all right?"

"Yes," she said, past the lump of terror high in her throat. She looked at him. His face was white, his eyes deep, dark pools. "Are you?"

"Yeah, I'm fine." He flashed a reassuring smile, squeezed her hand again before putting it into her lap. "Let me just see if the car's okay. The last thing we need is to have somebody come around that curve and straight into us." Jake turned the key, held his breath until the engine caught and purred. "Damn," he said roughly, as he swung the car back into the lane and edged forward, "we almost bought it, that time."

Emily nodded. "I know. I'm sorry, Jake. I—I guess I wasn't thinking. It was stupid to yell like that."

"No need to apologize." He shot her a quick smile. "Nobody wants to kill Bambi."

"Bambi?"

"Uh-huh." Jake leaned forward, peered intently out the windshield. The wipers were working as hard as they could but the snow was too heavy for any real visibility. The turn-off that led to his driveway was just a little further up the road. He could only hope the guy he paid to keep it plowed had already been there. "You'd think the deer would have finally figured it out by now, wouldn't you? That running across the road in front of a car isn't a good idea?"

"Oh." Emily bit her lip. "I didn't see a deer." Her voice was soft and small. "I just—I just…" She took a breath. "I thought about what we were doing. And I decided it was a mistake."

Jake took his eyes off the road long enough to stare at her. "Excuse me?"

"I said—"

"I heard what you said. I just don't believe it. You're telling me you almost got us killed because you suddenly decided you wanted to go home?"

"It wasn't sudden. I've been thinking about it for a while. And how was I supposed to know you'd react by almost crashing the car into a tree?"

"Oh, forgive me." His words were thick with sarcasm. "The next time I'm driving blind through a storm and the person seated next to me yells 'Stop,' I'll just keep going and hope for the best."

Emily lifted her chin. "I said I was sorry, didn't I?"

"You'd be sorrier if we were lying dead back there."

"Look, what I did was stupid. But I meant what I said, Jake. I want to go back to New York."

Jake gave a short, sharp laugh. "Yeah? Well, trust me, lady. So do I."

Emily's heart felt as if somebody were crushing it, which was even stupider than yelling "Stop." She'd already known

Jake had regrets. Why should it upset her, to hear him confirm it?

"Fine," she said coolly. "That makes the decision unanimous."

"It damned well does. Unfortunately, neither your vote nor mine counts. This blizzard owns the ballot box."

"This isn't a blizzard." Her voice wobbled a little and she cleared her throat. "I'll bet you never saw a blizzard in your life. Back home, in Rochester—"

"Trust me. We had blizzards in Pennsylvania, too."

Pennsylvania? Not New York? Was that where he was from? It was impossible to picture Jake living anywhere but in the elegant canyons of the city. She wanted to ask him where he'd grown up, and how, and what he'd been like as a boy...

But she wouldn't.

What was the matter with her tonight? You didn't ask questions like that of a man who'd just told you he was sorry he'd asked you to sleep with him.

"The wind has to blow at least thirty-five miles an hour for a snowstorm to be a blizzard," she said, blanking her mind to everything but the night and the storm. "And the visibility—"

Blah, blah, blah, Jake thought grimly. There she went, the Emily he knew, who could quote you chapter and verse on everything and anything—except how to be a woman.

He gritted his teeth, tuned her out, and concentrated on the road. There it was, just ahead. The turnoff. And yes, the guy had cleared it. He signaled for a right turn, not that there was anybody in back of him. Who'd be fool enough to be out on a night like this?

Only a man who'd been letting his gonads lead him around for the past week.

Well, no more.

He'd had lots of time to think, the past few hours, and what he'd thought was how dumb this whole escapade was.

He'd set out on a mission of mercy, been snared by his own hormones, and now he was taking a woman to the last place he'd ever thought he'd take a woman.

Not just a woman. Emily. Emily, for God's sake, who probably thought sex was another word for romance and love and lace-trimmed Valentine's Day cards. He'd backed himself into a corner he was going to have trouble getting out of, and for what? For a couple of hours in bed?

Jake almost laughed.

He could have taken the prim and proper Miss Taylor to bed one hundred and sixty miles ago. Back in the city, at his place. Or at hers. Or at some damned hotel, in a suite overlooking Central Park, if that was her preference. He could have had her anyplace but here, in a house that was his own personal hideaway from the real world.

He didn't want her here. He didn't want any woman here but, thanks to a momentary lapse in judgment, he sure as hell had one. And, as if that weren't bad enough, it looked as if they might end up stuck here for at least part of tomorrow.

What would they talk about? What would they do when the sex was over? It wasn't as if he'd never spent a whole weekend with a woman but it had always been in a place where there were things to do so you didn't have to sit around, looking at each other. Besides, those women knew how to play the game.

Emily didn't. She'd expect... What? Earnest conversation? An exchange of life stories?

Jake bit back a groan.

And come Monday morning, what would his life be like? Could he still walk into the office and greet her as if they were nothing more than two people who happened to work together?

No. Dammit, no. Women weren't like that. They put on a good act, said they were the same as men, said sex was sex and that it didn't have to be confused with love. And, he supposed, some of them even meant it.

Not Emily. Certainly, not Emily.

She was naïve to a fault. She'd probably only been with a couple of men. Every instinct warned him that she'd turn this one night into more than it was, more than he'd ever meant it to be. If he'd had himself under control, he'd have figured that out a lot sooner.

And that was another thing. He didn't like the feeling he had when he was around her, as if he weren't quite in charge of his own destiny, because he was.

Of course he was.

If only the roads were clear. If only the snow weren't coming down. If only he'd thought of all this before he'd asked her to come with him, before he'd started dreaming about her and yeah, okay, he dreamed about her, and wasn't that a laugh? What kind of man had dreams like that, when he knew that there were a dozen beautiful women just waiting to do in reality what Emily only did in those dreams?

Jake glared out the windshield. The house was just ahead. Normally, he felt good just at the sight of it, but not tonight. One huge master suite with an oversized tub and shower, a den, a living room, a half bath the Realtor had insisted on calling a powder room, and a country kitchen.

It was plenty big enough for him, but for him and a woman? For him and Emily?

It was too late for turning back but not too late for regrets.

Jake reached to the dashboard, depressed the button for the automatic garage door opener. The doors rolled up; he drove the Corvette inside and shut off the engine. Okay. Time to make the best of a bad situation.

"Well," he said, trying for pleasant and not quite making it, "here we are."

Emily wrenched open her door. "Thank you for telling me," she said coldly. "I'd never have figured it out if you hadn't."

Jake sighed. Oh, yeah. It was going to be a memorable

night. It was just a good thing the sofa in the den was comfortable.

He walked ahead of her, unlocked the door that led from the garage into the kitchen. The house was dark and cold. He was half tempted to leave it that way. It suited his mood. But he did the right thing, turned up the thermostat, then went from room to room, switching on lights before returning to the kitchen.

Emily was still standing where he'd left her, her back to him. Jake thawed, just a little. She looked lost, small and lonely...

No, she didn't. She turned around and she looked as if she'd been carved from the icicles that dangled from the eaves.

Okay, fine. That was the way she wanted it, that was the way it would be.

"I'll bring in your things," he snapped.

"What things? You mean, the stuff you bought today?"

"Yes."

"Don't bother. None of that's mine. You picked it, you paid for it. You can return it."

Jake peeled off his gloves, stuck them in the pockets of his leather jacket. "We've been all through this, remember? In Saks."

"How could I forget? You made such a scene..."

"I simply said you were to consider the clothes a gift."

"And I," Emily said sharply, "told you that I wouldn't."

"Dammit, I am not going through this again. Buying all that stuff was my—"

Emily unbuttoned her coat and shrugged it off. Jake swallowed dryly. He'd almost forgotten how she looked in that rose-colored dress and those high-heeled leather boots.

"It was my idea," he continued. "And it's a ridiculous thing to quarrel over. You'd never have done all that shopping if I—if I hadn't—"

"What's the matter?"

"Nothing." Nothing, unless he kept wondering what she had on under the dress. How come he hadn't thought of that before? How come he hadn't seen any underwear going in and out of that fitting room?

"Well, I'm not keeping the clothes."

"Yes, you are."

"No, I'm not."

"You are, and that's the end of it." Jake ripped off his jacket and tossed it on a chair. What did it matter, what she was wearing under the dress? He didn't care. For all he gave a damn, she could be wearing red flannel long johns. "I'm going to start a fire. How about you check out the kitchen and see if you can rustle up something to eat?"

"Oh, I see. You're the man, so you get to build the fire. I'm the woman, so I get to open a can of soup."

Jake threw out his arms. "You want to start the fire? Great. Be my guest. I'll be more than happy to switch jobs."

Emily lifted her chin. "I'd just as soon do the cooking, thank you. Why risk ptomaine poisoning, at your hands?"

She turned on her heel. Jake glared at her. "Women," he muttered, and then he marched into the living room, squatted down before the fireplace, and set to work.

Half an hour later, Jake sat on the carpet, cross-legged, before a roaring fire.

He was feeling a little better. A good fire always did that for him. And there were interesting smells coming from the direction of the kitchen.

He sighed, thought about the endless hours that lay ahead and figured it probably made sense to make the best of them. So he added another log to the blaze, got to his feet, headed for the wooden wine rack at the far end of the room, and frowned.

Red or white? He had no idea what Emily was cooking and he didn't much feel like invading her territory to ask. It was peaceful right now; why spoil things with a question about wine?

Red, he decided. Red seemed to suit a cold, snowy night.

Jake opened a bottle of Merlot, sniffed the cork and decided he'd made a good choice. Mmm. What was she making in there? Whatever it was, it smelled wonderful. His stomach gave an anticipatory growl. Damn, he was hungry. Starved, was a better word, but then all he'd had for breakfast was that bagel. Now that he thought about it, they'd managed to blow right past lunch.

Well, that figured. Why would he have thought of lunch, when his sparrow had been turning into a songbird, right before his eyes?

Jake plucked a pair of wineglasses from the shelf.

The truth was, she'd always been a songbird. She'd just managed to keep it hidden from the world. You didn't see the real Emily until you took a long look. A long, wonderful look. Then you realized that she was beautiful.

Jake poured the wine.

More beautiful than any woman he knew, and maybe part of the reason was that she didn't think so.

But she was. That soft mouth. Those dark, drown-in-me eyes. That elegant little nose, the incredible hair, the lovely, curvy body... And her smile. Her laugh, so open and easy. Her honesty, her intelligence, her lack of pretension...

The amazing thing was that Pete Archer had seen the real Emily right away, despite the fact that Archer was an ass. So had Thad Jennett. And now Eric had been added to her list of admirers. Eric, who probably had his hands in the hair of more gorgeous women in a day than most men did in a year...

Was he the only guy who'd been so blind?

Jake picked up the glasses of wine and headed for the kitchen.

Emily was at the stove. She'd put on the denim apron he'd bought for himself but never quite found the courage to use, even though it said Chef on the front in bright red letters. The apron was enormous on her; the sides overlapped in the middle of her back. She was stirring something in a big pot. That was what he'd smelled and now he sniffed the air again, smiling appreciatively at the mingled aromas of garlic, tomatoes and—

"Sausage?"

Emily spun around. Heat from the stove had flushed her cheeks; steam from the pot had turned her hair into a riotous mane of curls and she had a smear of something red on her chin.

Jake felt something twist around his heart.

Beautiful, he thought, Emily, you're so beautiful...

He stiffened. Okay, so she was beautiful. So were a million other women. And there wasn't a reason in the world to get into an affair with her when he knew it would end badly.

Jake fixed a smile to his lips and strolled towards her.

"Vino for the cook," he said briskly, "but only if you tell me that really is sausage I smell."

She hesitated. He could almost see her weighing the benefits and drawbacks of a temporary thaw. After a few seconds, she gave him a little smile and accepted the glass he offered her. A truce had been declared, at least for the moment.

"It is," she said. "You said to poke around the kitchen. Well, I did—and I found some sausage in the freezer."

"You could have found a mastodon, and it wouldn't surprise me. I bought the freezer when I bought the house, filled it—and never opened it again." He held out his glass. "Salud."

They touched glasses. Emily took a sip of wine.

"Mmm. That's lovely."

"I'm glad you like it. I wasn't sure what your preferences are."

"Except when it comes to cephalopod mollusks."

Jake grinned. "Dangerous things, those mollusks."

"Mmm." She drank some of her wine. "Actually, I don't know much about wines. I just know what I like."

"Yes. So do I."

Their eyes met and held. Emily's color deepened and she turned away. "Anyway," she said, "I found the sausage. There were some canned tomatoes in one of the cupboards, along with a box of spaghetti. And you had garlic and cheese in the fridge, so I figured I'd make a sauce. It won't be anywhere near as good as that stuff at *La Gondola,* but—"

"How could it be?" Jake leaned back against a granite-topped counter and crossed his feet at the ankles. "I mean, heck, without some tentacles and a blob of ink, who'd want to eat spaghetti?"

Emily laughed. "Who, indeed?"

"Is the sauce going to take a while to simmer? We had a neighbor when I was a kid, lady named of Mrs. Rossini. She used to make this terrific sauce—it would make the whole street smell great. I remember it took forever to cook."

"Oh, this won't take that long. Just another half hour or so."

"Good. 'Cause I'm as hungry as a bear."

Emily picked up a wooden spoon and stirred the sauce. "So, where was this, where Mrs. Rossini used to make her sauce? Pennsylvania?"

"Uh-huh. How'd you know that?"

She shrugged. "You mentioned Pennsylvania before, when we were in the car."

"Ah. Yeah, Pennsylvania. That's where I grew up."

"I've never been there."

"Not much to see in my part of it," Jake said, and smiled. "Trees, trees, more trees...and coal mines."

"Coal mines, huh? That sounds interesting."

"It isn't," Jake said flatly. He stepped away from the counter. "Looks as if we have just enough time to sit by the fire and enjoy our wine."

"All right," she said, after a second's hesitation. "That would be nice."

Yes, he thought, yes, it would be. Sitting beside the fire, his arm around her shoulders, her head on his chest...

Jake put down his glass. "The thing is," he said gruffly, "I'm not a guy who believes in forever after."

He spoke before he could stop himself, because the words needed saying, but if he'd taken Emily by surprise, she didn't show it.

"I know that, Jake."

"Do you? I want you, Emily. Hell, I want you so badly it makes me ache." He took a slow step towards her. "But I don't want to hurt you. And I'm not sure what you expect out of tonight."

Emily didn't have to think about her answer. She'd come to grips with reality while she'd been making the sauce. She was an adult and so was he. Oh, she'd tried to pretty things up by telling herself she wasn't a woman meant for a one-night stand but the truth was, just as the sauce was made up of a bit of this and a bit of that, so was life.

Tonight was about sex, not romance. That was fine. She didn't believe in romance, anyway. This—being with Jake, learning what other women knew—was part of life. And here, at long last, was her chance to live it.

"Just tonight," she said softly, her chin level, her eyes steady on his. "That's all I expect, Jake. I just want—I want what you said you'd give me. What you said you'd teach me."

She sounded calm, almost cool. She wasn't, though. Jake could see the glass trembling in her hand. She was afraid, and excited, and the knowledge that she was both sent a lightning bolt of anticipation through his blood.

He took her wineglass from her hand and set it aside.

"Come here," he said softly, and drew her to him. "Em." He ran his hands down her back, then up again. "Em, you're so lovely."

"You don't have to lie to me. I know I'm not—"

Her voice was shaking. Well, why wouldn't it? She was terrified. Where was she supposed to put her hands? What was she supposed to do and say?

Her breath caught. Jake had nuzzled her hair aside. His mouth was hot against her neck.

"It's true, though," he whispered. "You're beautiful, and sweet, and perfect."

"Jake." Emily shut her eyes. "I don't—I don't know what you want me to do."

He took her hands, looped them behind his neck. "Just do whatever you want to do, sweetheart."

"Yes, but I—I—"

He kissed her gently, the brush of his lips against hers like a feather against her skin. Emily caught her breath.

"Jake? I don't think…"

"Good." He put his hand under her chin, tipped her face up to his. "Don't think, Em. That's it. Don't think. Just feel."

His eyes were deep and dark; she knew she could tumble into them, get lost in them forever. "Jake? Maybe we were right the first time. That coming here was a mis—"

He kissed her again. His lips pressed hers more firmly this time but his mouth was soft. Soft, and cool, and wonderful.

Her heart began to race. And there was a strange tingling sensation low in her belly.

"Jake. Jake, listen. I said that maybe coming here was—"

He silenced her by fitting his mouth carefully over hers, stroking the tip of his tongue against the seam of her lips.

"Emily," he said gruffly, "just turn off that brain of yours and kiss me back."

She did. She wrapped her arms around his neck, kissed him, and knew, at long last, that being here, with Jake, being in his arms, was what she'd waited for, all her life.

Jake groaned as she opened her mouth to him. He cupped her face in his hands, accepted her invitation, delved into the heat and sweetness of her mouth. Emily moaned, lifted herself to him, against him, pressed her soft, soft body against the hardness of his.

"Emily," he said, and he lifted her into his arms, carried her into the living room, to the fireplace, before he lowered her to her feet.

She'd knotted the apron; he'd always been good at knots, he thought incongruously, hell, he'd almost been a Boy Scout when he was a kid. He'd have sewn a hundred merit badges on his shirt if his mother ever had enough money for the cost of the uniform. But his hands were shaking now; it took forever to undo the knot and get the apron off.

Ah, he was right. She was beautiful. The rose-colored dress matched the color in her face. Her eyes were dark pools, wide with expectation and wonder. Her breasts were high, the nipples hard and visible beneath the soft wool.

"Em," he whispered.

He watched her face as he lifted his hand, brushed his thumb over the distended bit of wool. She cried out; her head fell back and Jake caught her, gathered her close, eased the dress off one creamy shoulder and pressed his mouth to her flesh, to the pulse racing in the hollow of her throat. She smelled of roses and sweet cream; she tasted of honey and heaven, and he told himself to go slow, go slow...

How could he?

The blood was pounding in his veins. And Emily... Emily was whispering his name as he cupped her breast, teased it to life.

"Please," she said, "Jake, please..."

He could feel the room spinning around him. She was crooning to him, begging him, arching against him. She tugged his shirt out of his jeans, ran her hands up his back.

Go slow, he told himself fiercely, dammit, go slow...

"Jake?" she said, and touched him. Touched his erection as it strained against his jeans, and he was lost. Lost, to everything but needing her, wanting her, having her.

"Take me," she said. "Please, Jake. Come inside me, now."

Jake growled. He pulled her down to the carpet before the fire, thrust his hands under her skirt, felt the whisper of silk on her thighs, the slickness of silk between them.

She was wet and hot. Wet and hot, for him.

The world, and all his reason, disappeared.

"Now," he said, and he ripped away the wet silk, opened his fly, freed himself and thrust deep, thrust hard...

And felt the barrier, the one he'd never, in his entire life, encountered. Stunned, he held still. Tried to think. To pull back. Emily wouldn't let him. She dug her hands into his shoulders, dragged him down to her, lifted herself to him.

"Em," he said, "Em, wait..."

Too late. She thrust her hips forward and impaled herself on his hard flesh.

A moment of shimmering pain, and then Jake was inside her, deep inside her, and she knew, she knew why she'd let this happen, why she'd wanted it to happen.

"Jake," Emily whispered, " oh, Jake, I..."

Jake groaned, thrust one last time, and the world came apart in a shattering explosion of light.

CHAPTER NINE

JAKE buried his face in Emily's throat, kissed her damp skin, then rolled onto his side and curved her tightly against him.

"Em." He looked deep into her eyes. "Are you all right?"

All right? She was wonderful. Her body tingled; her skin felt flushed and hot. Was she supposed to tell him that?

"Baby," he said, drawing her closer and running his hand gently up and down her spine, "sweetheart, I'm sorry."

"For what? I wanted… I wanted you to make love to me, Jake."

"Yeah." A teasing smile angled across his lips. "Oh, yeah, Em. I know that." Jake threaded his fingers into her hair, brought her mouth to his for a long, tender kiss.

What did he mean, he knew she'd wanted him to make love to her? Yes, of course he knew. She'd told him. But there was something in that little smile…

"Really," she said quickly, "it was—it was fine, just the way you did it."

"Fine, huh?" He laughed softly. "Is that the best you can do?"

His tone was gentle. He was teasing her, she knew, just as she knew she should make some equally teasing response. She couldn't. Her heart was still racing but her mind was blank. There had to be a protocol for this but for the life of her, she had no idea what it was. Did you say thank you to the man who'd just shown you ecstasy? Or did you just lie here and wonder where this magic had been, all your adult life?

Nothing she'd read, nothing she'd imagined, had prepared her for the reality of what had just happened. The feeling of Jake, deep within her. His hot skin. His clever mouth. His slow hands. She didn't want to ruin it now, by saying the wrong thing. As it was, she'd come close to doing just that. She'd almost said…almost said…

She'd almost said, Jake, I love you. And she didn't. Of course, she didn't. She'd just been so overwhelmed by sensation…

"Em, talk to me." Jake eased her onto her back and leaned over her, his weight on his elbows as he looked into her face. "Did I hurt you? I know I went too fast. I'm sorry. I couldn't…" He took a breath, laid his forehead against hers. "You should have told me," he said softly.

"Told you…"

Heat flooded her face. That she was a virgin. That was what he meant. And he was right. She probably should have. Jake was accustomed to being with women who knew about sex. He'd signed on to teach her about passion, not to spend a night with a trembling novice.

"I'm sorry," she whispered, and closed her eyes. "I guess I should have, but—"

"I'd have slowed down, if I'd known." He gave a little laugh. "At least, I'd have tried." He took her face in his hands, brushed his lips over hers. "To be honest, I don't know if I could have. I wanted you so badly, Em. And when you let me know you felt the same way…"

"I did?"

"Uh-huh." Jake kissed her again, and she felt his lips turn up in a smile against hers. "'Take me,' you said. 'Come inside me,' you said. What man could think straight, after that?"

Take me? Come inside me? Had she…could she possibly have…Emily felt a stab of anguish. Yes. Yes, she had. That was what he'd meant when he gave her that smug little smile. She'd said all that. She'd begged him.

And now, she wanted to die of embarrassment.

She'd done everything wrong. She'd pleaded for him to take her, made him come too quickly, been a virgin when a virgin was the last thing a man like Jake would expect. And she'd come within an inch of saying she loved him when, of course, she didn't.

Perfect, she thought. An absolutely perfect debut, Emily. Too bad there was nothing left for an encore.

"Jake."

"Mmm?"

He was kissing her throat, lightly nipping her skin. And she, dammit, she was getting aroused again. She could feel it happening: the liquid rush deep inside, the tingle in her breasts...

"Jake, let me up, please."

"In a minute."

He moved lazily, settled himself lower on her body, kissed the rise of her breast. "You have too much clothing on," he said huskily. "Does this dress have a zipper?"

Her dress. Oh, it was worse and worse. She still had her dress on, even her boots. Jake was fully clothed, too. She hadn't even given him the chance to—

"Jake. I want to get up!"

There was a note of panic in her voice. She heard it; she knew Jake did, too, from the way he reacted.

"I *did* hurt you." He drew back. "Em, baby, I'm sorry. I—"

"Dammit, will you stop saying that?" Her face flamed. "Look, I don't want to talk about it. I just—I want you to get off me." He did, and she shot to her feet. "Where's the bathroom?"

"Down the hall, but I can make things better, if you'd just—"

She didn't let him finish. Instead, she tugged the bodice of her dress up and the hem of it down. She could feel Jake's eyes boring into her as she made her way down the hall. Maybe it was just as well she was still dressed. Walking away naked, with him watching, would have been the final humiliation.

Why had she come here? Why had she done this? She'd never be able to look at Jake again, without thinking—

Emily slammed the bathroom door behind her and locked it.

"Oh my God," she said, in a choked whisper.

After a few seconds, she turned on the light, took a steadying breath and faced herself in the mirror. It was worse than she'd expected. Her hair was a tangle of wild curls, her lip gloss was gone, her mascara was smudged. She looked like a woman who'd been doing exactly what she'd been doing...except she hadn't been doing it very well.

A sound burst from her throat. Turning on the water muffled it; she cupped her hands under the stream. It was icy-cold; she gasped as she splashed it on her face.

Now what?

If only this were New York, she thought, as she dried her hands and face. *Thank you for everything, Jake,* she'd say. *No, no, don't get up. I'll see myself out.* Two minutes later, she'd be in the street, hailing a taxi or finding the nearest bus stop or subway station. Forget the snowstorm. Snowstorms didn't stop anybody, in the city.

But she wasn't in the city. No buses, no taxis, no subways. She might as well have been on the moon.

"Em?"

Emily spun around and stared at the door.

The knob rattled. "Baby, are you okay?"

Baby. What kind of name was that for a man to call a woman?

"Yes," she said brightly, "I'm fine."

"You don't sound fine. Are you crying?"

"Don't be silly." Emily swiped at her streaming eyes with the back of her hand. She *was* crying. And wasn't that dumb? Okay, so she'd made a fool of herself but still, why would she cry? "Why would I cry, Jake?"

"I don't know, but I'd like to find out. Open the door, Emily."

"No."

"Emily." Jake's voice hardened. "Open this door!"

"I don't have to. This is a bathroom. People are entitled to privacy, in a bathroom."

Jake leaned his forehead against the door. Dammit, now what? Of course she was crying. He'd dealt with enough teary females to know what a woman sounded like when she was crying. It usually sent him running in the opposite direction but where could he run to? This was his house, the wind and the snow were howling outside…and besides, it was doing funny things to him, hearing his sparrow weep.

Why would she cry? Okay, things hadn't been perfect. He hadn't made love to her the way he'd intended, so that it would last, so that he could seek out all her most sensitive places, hold her in his arms and watch her lovely face as she found the fulfillment he, and only he, could bring her…

He, and only he?

Jake frowned. What in hell was that supposed to mean? He was teaching Emily about passion. That was what he'd promised, what she'd accepted.

Easy. He needed a minute to get things in perspective. What had happened had thrown him. He'd expected Emily to be inexperienced, but a virgin?

No way.

That had come as a shock. No wonder he'd—he'd—

Who was he kidding? He'd lost control. That had never happened to him before, not since he was a kid. He loved sex: the musky scents; the hot, whispered sounds; the swift rocket-ride to the stars, but a little piece of him always stayed outside, kind of like an observer. What had happened to that observer this time? How come, at the end, nothing had mattered but being deep inside Emily?

The answer was simple. All that prim propriety, hiding all that heat. What man wouldn't lose control? What man wouldn't find the experience exceptional?

In fact, he wanted her again. Right now. The truth was, he

hadn't stopped wanting her, even after they'd both come. Did she know how rare that was, that a man and a woman found release at the same instant? No. She wouldn't know. She was so innocent. So...

Jake rubbed his hands over his face. His body was hardening, his pulse starting to do the samba, because he wanted to make love to Emily again. And what did Emily want?

She wanted to lock herself inside the powder room and cry.

Had he failed her that badly?

"Emily," he said, trying to sound stern, "I want you out of there this second."

Silence greeted his demand. He frowned, eyed the door narrowly.

"Em? Come out. I'll bust the door down, if I have to."

Emily gave a ladylike snort. "Oh, that's the ticket, Jake. You don't get what you want, just start barking!"

"Dammit, Emily..." A nerve ticked in Jake's temple. He laid his palms flat against the door, touched his forehead to the wood. "Let's not turn this into a battle. Just open the lock, okay?"

"No."

"You have to, sooner or later."

"I don't."

"Of course you do. You'll get hungry, or tired or thirsty..."

"I'm not hungry. There's plenty of water and I can always curl up on the floor."

Jake looked at the door, considered beating his head against it, and decided Emily would simply stand by and let him do it.

"Em?"

"Yes?"

He hesitated. "Are you sure I didn't hurt you?"

"Positive." She spoke softly, so softly that he could hardly hear her. "You didn't hurt me at all."

Jake cleared his throat. "Yeah, but I disappointed you."

"You didn't disappoint me, either."

"Sure, I did. I was—I was way too fast. I didn't mean it to be like that but when you said—"

"Don't repeat it!" Emily closed her eyes in misery. "I know what I said. If I could take it back—"

"Take back that you wanted me inside you?"

"Please," she whispered, "don't talk about it. I'm so embarrassed…"

"Embarrassed? That you let me know you wanted me? Em, don't you know what that did to me? Hearing you say those things?"

Emily slid down to the floor and leaned her head against the door. "You don't have to be polite, Jake."

Jake gave a choked laugh as he slid to the floor on the opposite side of the door. "Hell, Sparrow, good manners have nothing to do with this. I'm just sorry I made it all so quick. I wanted it to be perfect."

"It *was* perfect. It's just that I… What did you call me?"

"Sparrow. My sweet, hot little sparrow."

Emily cringed. "'Hot' isn't a word a lady appreciates, Jake."

"A woman's not supposed to be a lady when a man makes love to her, Em."

"No?"

"No. Is that what this is all about? That you weren't a lady?"

Another long silence. "Maybe."

"Baby, listen to me. A lady's the last thing a man wants in his bed."

He waited. She didn't reply.

"Emily? Sweetheart, please open the door. I promise, next time will be better."

"There won't be a next time." She paused. "And—and even if there were, how could it be better?" She thought back to that hot explosion of light. "How could it?" she said again, but very softly.

Jake rose slowly to his feet. "Open the door," he said huskily, "and I'll show you."

He waited. After a few seconds, he heard a sound, a soft rustle of clothing. The door opened a crack. Emily peered out.

"I think it would be best if I went home now."

Jake's smile tilted. "How're you going to manage that, Sparrow? Do you have a toboggan parked outside?"

She opened the door wider and stepped into the hall. Jake's heart did that funny upside down thing in his chest again. Her new hairdo was a mess, her lip gloss was all kissed off and the artfully applied mascara had dried into raccoonlike smudges under her teary eyes.

She was beautiful.

"Just look at you," he said gruffly. He took a step forward, gently dried her tears with his thumbs. "You've ruined all that goo that woman spent hours putting on your face."

"It wasn't goo," she said, sniffling a little but managing to sound defiant anyway, "and she spent two minutes."

Jake took her hand. "Come sit by the fire with me."

"I'd really like to go home."

"Yeah, well, you can't."

He led her into the living room. What he really wanted was to pull her into his arms, kiss her until she trembled and begged him to make love to her again, but he wouldn't do it. This was the time for seduction. Yeah, he'd seduce her. Slowly. Tenderly. Until she was on fire for him, the way he was on fire for her.

He sat down on the sofa, tried to pull her into his lap, but she wouldn't let him.

"I'd rather sit in the chair."

"How am I going to kiss you if I'm sitting here and you're sitting in the chair?"

"Jake. You said you'd teach me…things. And you have. You already—"

He tugged harder. She tumbled into his lap and he silenced her with a kiss. His mouth was warm; the tip of his tongue teased her lips. She swayed towards him, moaned, then pulled back.

"No," she said, a little breathlessly, "once was enough. Honestly, Jake—"

"Honestly, Sparrow," he whispered, as his hands spanned her waist, "once is never enough."

"It is. It was. And then there's our supper. The sauce, and the pasta…"

"To hell with supper," Jake said in a husky whisper that made her breath quicken. "Kiss me, Em."

When she didn't, he kissed her, instead, and slipped his tongue into her mouth. The heat of it, the taste of him, made her dizzy.

"Jake." She leaned her forehead against his. "Jake, stop. You make me feel—you make me feel—"

"What? Tell me. I want to know." His hands cupped her face, tilted it to his. "I want to know what you like. What things you want me to do."

Everything, she thought, oh, Jake, everything.

"This?" he said, and kissed her again. "And this?" he whispered, and cupped her breasts in his hands. "This, too," he murmured, and ran his thumbs over her nipples. "Ah, Sparrow, Sparrow, I want you so badly…"

Emily moaned, put her arms around Jake's neck and kissed him. She wanted him, too. Wanted his mouth, his hands, his body. Wanted his soul, and his heart…

Suddenly, she tore her mouth from his. "No," she gasped, and scrambled to her feet, but Jake went after her, put his arms around her, drew her back against his chest.

"Yes," he whispered, and buried his face in the soft, sweet place where her neck and shoulder joined.

She fell back against him, lifted her arm and lay her hand

against his cheek. Her fingers skimmed across his lips. He caught them, sucked them into the heat of his mouth as he undid the zipper that ran down the back of her dress. He wrapped a handful of her hair around his fist, dragged it aside and kissed the nape of her neck.

Her skin was like silk. He wanted to tear the dress away, feast on her with all his senses. Instead, he eased the dress to her waist and covered her breasts with his hands, teased the crests with his thumbs, felt her tremble, shudder, felt his body turning into steel.

"Do you like that?" he whispered.

Emily's breath caught. "Yes. Oh, yes. I—I—"

He turned her in his arms, took her mouth with his, nipped at her bottom lip until her mouth opened and he could slip his tongue inside. She trembled, pressed herself against him, and he shuddered with almost savage exaltation.

She was his. His, and no other man's. She had never belonged to anyone else and she never…

His mind whirled, teetered on the brink of a dangerous chasm. But Emily was holding him, kissing him, whispering his name and he couldn't think, couldn't do anything but feel.

He kissed her, hard, tilted her head back as he took possession of her mouth. The dress tore under his hands as he slid down her body. It pooled at her feet and he saw Emily, his Emily, for the very first time.

She was every dream he'd ever had, and every hope. Her body was slender, her curves feminine, her skin flushed with desire. She was wearing lace. White lace. Bra, tiny panties, stockings that ended at her thighs. White, all of it, as soft and pure as the snow.

But her boots were black. Black as midnight, black as sin, tight, sleek and high on her legs.

Jake shuddered again, knotted his hands, swore to himself that he would make this second time perfect.

He bent to her and put his mouth against hers, holding her captive only with his kiss. Then he knelt and eased the boots from her feet, one at a time, pausing to kiss her ankle, her arch. He heard her make a whispered sound, felt the brush of her hand against his hair as he rose and he paused at the juncture of her thighs, told himself again to go slow, go slow, not to frighten her...

"Em," he whispered, and his hands closed around the backs of her thighs as he pressed his face against the white lace panties.

Her cry of pleasure was almost his undoing. He could feel the heat, the dampness of her through the lace; the woman-scent of her arousal was perfume to his soul. His sparrow was trembling with desire and it was all for him.

For him, he thought, and he stood straight and gathered her into his arms.

"You're beautiful," he said softly, "so beautiful that you make my heart stop."

She looked at him through those wide, dark eyes. "You are, too. I never knew a man could be beautiful, Jake."

"Do you want to see more of me, Sparrow?"

The tip of her tongue snaked across her bottom lip. "Yes," she said. "Yes, please."

Eyes locked to hers, Jake unbuttoned his shirt. It fell open and Emily's breath hitched. It was true. He *was* beautiful. All that taut muscle. The tanned skin. The whorls of black, silky hair...

She reached out a hand, hesitated, started to pull it back but Jake clasped her wrist, put her palm flat against his chest. He caught his breath; she gave a little hum of pleasure. His skin felt hot, his body hard. Without thinking, she leaned forward and pressed her lips to the strong column of his throat.

Jake trembled. "Oh Lord, Em," he whispered, and for the first time in her life, she knew what it meant to have a man want her. No. Not just a man. Jake. Jake, who she...

She jerked back, would have spun away, but he caught her shoulders, pulled her close and kissed her. There was nothing gentle about the kiss. His mouth was rough and demanding, the stroke of his tongue possessive, and Emily let it happen, the feeling that her bones were melting, that Jake was taking her, claiming her, that he was marking her as his own...

That she loved him.

She loved Jake McBride. She loved everything about him. His beautiful face. His powerful body. His intelligence, his humor, his hot temper and now, his heart-stopping passion.

No. No! She didn't want to love Jake. She didn't want to love any man, especially not one who was everything she'd sworn to avoid, everything her sisters had foolishly thought fascinating. Jake was too handsome, too macho, too reckless, too restless...

Emily caught her breath.

It was too late for thought or for regrets. Jake was touching her. Opening her bra. Claiming her breasts as they tumbled into his waiting hands. Sucking her nipples. Licking them while he eased her panties down her hips, down her legs.

She cried out, clasped Jake's shoulders for support. He said her name, tore off his clothes, swept her into his arms and took her down with him, in front of the fire.

"Jake," she said, her voice trembling with emotion, her hands clasping his face.

"Don't be afraid, Em," he whispered.

She wasn't afraid. Not of Jake. She was afraid of what she felt, what she wanted, what she could never have.

"Please," she said, "Jake, please."

Emily opened her arms. Jake groaned, parted her thighs and sank deep, deep, deep into softness. The sweet softness that belonged only to him.

The softness of Emily.

CHAPTER TEN

THE snow continued all through the night.

Jake and Emily fell asleep before the fire, awoke and made love again.

Afterwards, he carried her to his bed.

"Mmm," she sighed, as he gathered her close against him under the soft down comforter.

Jake kissed her, tucked her head against his shoulder, and they tumbled back into sleep. When he awoke next, it was morning and the sky, visible through the bedroom window, was a peaceful cerulean blue.

The storm was over, which meant the main roads leading back to New York were probably clear.

Jake looked at Emily, still sleeping in his arms.

But he hadn't heard the sound of a snowplow.

The highways could be as smooth as glass. It didn't matter. Until the guy who plowed his driveway and road showed up, he and his sparrow were snowbound. He knew, from past experience, that his house was last on the list.

What a pity, he thought, smiling again as he drew Emily closer.

She sighed. Her fingers spread just over his heart but she didn't wake. Good. He didn't want to disturb her. She was new to all this and she had to ache, just a little. Her muscles had to be sore.

But he knew how simple it would be, to wake her as he'd done during the night. He had only to kiss her, taste her mouth, savor its sweetness. Even asleep, her lips would part in response to his. Mmm, she'd say, Jake...and he'd say yes, Em, yes, baby, and her arms would tighten around him, her warm, naked body would move against his...

Oh, hell.

Jake bit back a groan, relaxed his hold on Emily and tried to put some distance between them, but she wouldn't let it happen. She made a soft sound of distress, burrowed against him, threw her leg across his.

"Emily." His voice was hoarse, and he cleared his throat. "Baby?"

"Mmm."

No. He couldn't. He wouldn't...

She shifted her leg higher. Jake caught his breath.

"Sparrow, just move away a little. Just..."

Emily opened her eyes. Jake watched as the blur of sleep gave way to awareness. A delicate blush rose in her cheeks.

"Jake," she whispered.

"Yes." He kissed her. Her mouth was warm and soft under his. "I didn't mean to wake you."

"Is it morning?"

"Uh-huh." He kissed her throat, inhaling the sweet woman-scent of her skin. "The storm's over."

"Then, we can head back to—" her voice broke as his mouth found her breast "—to New York."

"Not yet," he said softly, and drew her nipple gently between his teeth. "We're still snowed in." He lifted his head and looked at her. Desire had turned her eyes dark. Slowly, he moved over her, kissed and licked his way down her body.

"Jake," she whispered, "Jake, what—"

"I just want to kiss you. Here. Right..."

She cried out, put her hands in his hair, arched towards him. Jake groaned, slid his hands under her bottom, touched his mouth to her again, and she tumbled with him into a whirlpool of dazzling sensation.

It was late morning before Emily stirred again.

She knew it was late. Sunlight filled the room; she could hear the steady *pit-pat* of the icicles melting from the eaves.

She was alone in the rumpled bed. The bedroom door was open…and she could hear a male voice singing downstairs.

Emily smiled, rolled onto her belly and took Jake's pillow in her arms.

She didn't know much about rock and roll but either the radio stations in this part of the northeast featured really bad artists or Jake was singing his heart out. And, if he was, there wasn't a singer in the world who had anything to worry about.

Jake was no threat to them… He was only a threat to her.

Emily's smile faded. She sat up, her knees tenting the blankets, and ran her fingers through her tangled curls. The reality of morning sent the dreams of the night skittering into the shadows.

Sleeping with Jake hadn't been on the agenda. Neither had falling in love with him. But both had happened, and now…

And now, what? What was a woman supposed to do, the morning after she'd slept with a man?

"Oh, Lord," Emily whispered, and laid her head against her knees.

What had she done? Falling for Jake wasn't just foolish, it was disaster waiting to happen. He didn't love her. He didn't even want an affair with her. He'd been perfectly clear about that. He'd wanted to show her what sex was all about….

And he had.

The weekend would end, and so would everything else. Monday morning, she'd show up at the office. So would Jake. And…

And?

And, nothing would be the same. Jake would look at her but not the way he always had. He'd look at her the way he'd looked at Brandi. With sadness, or maybe with embarrassment…

Emily fell back against the pillows.

A woman who slept with her boss was a liability, but a

woman who fell in love with him was a calamity. How many times had she heard the same story? Secretaries, assistants, falling for the men they worked for. It happened with pathetic frequency, and always ended the same way, with the woman not just nursing a broken heart but doing it while she stood on the unemployment line.

Who was she kidding? The job was the least of it. It was Jake's inevitable rejection that would be what would kill her. She'd laughed at the way Brandi had pursued him but it wasn't quite so easy to laugh, now that she'd been with Jake, now that she'd fallen in love with him.

Okay. Emily drew a resolute breath. The thing to do was to end this, quickly. The snow had stopped. Even here, in the middle of nowhere, the roads would be clear. She'd dress, phone for a taxi, thank Jake politely for—for all his efforts...

"There you are, woman."

Emily sat up. Jake was standing in the doorway, a rakish smile on his lips. He wore jeans and a black T-shirt; his feet were bare, his hair hung over his forehead and the stubble on his jaw was dark and sexy-looking.

Just seeing him made her feel dizzy.

"I figured you were going to sleep the day away."

She drew the blanket to her chin and looked at the bedside clock. "I didn't—I didn't realize it was so late."

"Yeah." His voice softened, his smile tilted. "Well, you were tired."

Her eyes flashed to his. He was coming towards her, and the way he was looking at her made her blush.

"Jake," she said quickly, "I'm getting up."

"Yes, you are." He sat down next to her, on the bed. "You're absolutely getting up, considering that I've spent the past thousand hours making pancakes, bacon, sausages and toast."

"Bacon *and* sausages?" she said, smiling before she could stop herself.

"I didn't know which you preferred."

"Actually…" Emily sat straighter as she remembered her plan. "Actually, I think I'll skip breakfast."

"No way." Jake reached out, brushed a curl from her forehead. "Didn't you pay attention to your teachers, when you were a kid? It's the most important meal of the day."

"Yes, but—"

"Besides, you'll hurt my feelings."

"Jake, honestly—"

"Honestly, I'll think you're trying to get out of eating what I've cooked."

He looked crestfallen, and about as serious as a puppy caught with a sock in its teeth. Emily fought back the desire to laugh.

"It's very nice that you've cooked breakfast, but—"

"But, you have to get back to the city."

"No. I mean, yes. The roads must be clear by now."

Jake looped a finger under the edge of the blanket and tugged it off her shoulder.

"They are," he said softly. "Clear enough so we can go out for dinner. I made reservations at The Hilltop Inn. You'll love it."

"I can't stay. Really." Emily caught her breath. His mouth was on her throat, his teeth and beard rasping sexily against her skin. "Jake," she said weakly, "I have things to do."

He pushed the blanket to her waist. "Uh-huh. So do I."

"Horace needs…" Her breath hitched. "He needs fresh seed."

"Call Mrs. Levy," Jake whispered, as he stroked his hand over her naked hip. "She has a set of keys to your apartment."

"Mrs. Levy? How do you know…"

"She told me, while we were freezing on that stoop, waiting for you to ring the buzzer." Jake licked her belly, blew lightly on her damp skin. "She told me lots of things, Em. That you were sweet, and generous. That you were sexy and beautiful."

Emily's hands rose. She stroked Jake's hair, cupped his strong jaw.

"She didn't," she said, and laughed softly.

"Not the sexy and beautiful part, no." Jake parted her thighs, watched her face as he touched her, felt his heart leap as she moaned. "I found that out, all by myself."

"Oh. Oh, Jake, please..."

"Please, what?" he said in a husky whisper.

"Please make love to me," she sighed, and went into Jake's arms.

Nobody had ever asked Jake to describe himself but if someone had, he'd have said he was a normal, healthy, heterosexual male of the twenty-first century.

In other words, he thought as he sat across from Emily in a candlelit booth at an inn a few miles west of Litchfield, in other words, he'd been with his fair share of women. What the heck. Maybe more than his fair share. He'd taken them to dinner, to the theater, to concerts, to parties. And to bed.

"...and," Emily was saying, her eyes filled with laughter, "Angela said she wanted to be blonder, no matter what our mother said. So she locked herself in the bathroom. A little while later, we heard this awful screech..."

Oh, yes. An impressive number of women, to bed.

"...green. I mean, bright green, Jake! And Serena and I tried not to laugh, but..."

Except, it had never been an entire weekend in bed, now that he thought about it. Saturday night, maybe Sunday morning, and that was it. By noon, he was always feeling restless. By two, he was out the door.

"I could set my clock by you, Jake," Brandi had said, with a sad little laugh.

Well, it was true. Saturday night, Sunday morning—that was a weekend. Anything that stretched beyond that, the lady might get ideas that would complicate things.

Plus, there was the boredom factor.

What did you do, when the sex was over? What did you talk about?

Everything, as it turned out. Everything, if Emily was the lady.

They'd finally gotten around to breakfast, even though it was so cold they'd had to start all over, from scratch.

Don't throw all that food out, Emily had said. It's wasteful.

So he'd cut up the pancakes for the birds, the bacon and sausages for the raccoons, while she'd made eggs—over easy, as it turned out, exactly the way he liked them—and bacon, and biscuits from a box of mix he'd bought and buried in the depths of a kitchen cupboard.

Then they'd bundled up, gone outside, left breakfast for the birds and the raccoons in the back of the yard, near the tree line. And yes, he'd shown her the lot next door, had a serious discussion about its value until Emily had sighed and said well, its real value was in its beauty, at which point he'd hauled her into his arms and kissed her so that they'd stumbled back into the house, made love again, slept awhile, awakened, listened to CD's because, as it turned out, she didn't really hate all rock and roll and he didn't really hate all classical stuff...

And they'd talked.

He loved listening to her. She'd told him about her first few jobs, about her sisters—her incredibly beautiful sisters, she called them. About her first apartment, and about Horace. How she'd spotted him languishing in a dingy pet-shop window, his feathers all dirty and mussed. How she hadn't intended to buy a pet at all, but how she couldn't possibly have left him there...

"What were you like, as a little girl?"

Emily blinked. Jake had interrupted her in the middle of a sentence and it was as much a surprise to him as it was to her. But, all of a sudden, he wanted to know about the Emily who'd existed before she came to New York. He wanted to be able to see her, in his mind's eye, although he thought he already could. She'd have been delicate and shy, with a mane of untamed hair and a stack of books always in her arms.

"Well…" She hesitated. "Well, there was nothing special about me, Jake. Compared to my sisters, I—"

Jake reached for her hand. "You're the one I want to hear about."

"I was, um, I was small."

"Delicate," he said, and smiled.

"I was quiet."

"Shy," he said, and lifted her hand to his mouth.

"And I always had my nose in a book."

Jake grinned and laced his fingers through hers. "Tell me more."

"No, it's your turn. Tell me about you."

"There's nothing much to tell."

"Ah. You mean, Jacob McBride was born in a well-furnished office, wearing a custom-made suit?"

Jake thought of the tiny house he'd been raised in, of the patched clothes he'd worn until the fabrics were too worn to fix, and he laughed.

"Not by a long shot."

"Well, what then? Was your father a banker, or… What's so funny?"

"Nothing," Jake said. "Hell, it's not funny at all. It's just the thought of my old man as a banker in a custom-made suit. I never saw him wear anything but overalls and a flannel shirt except on Sundays." His smile tilted. "His day of rest, you know? And he'd spend it trying to figure out how to pay the bills…"

"Jake." Emily's fingers tightened over his. "I'm sorry."

"No, that's okay. He was a good man. I just don't usually…" He shrugged. "I don't talk about him much."

Emily nodded. Jake didn't talk about himself much, either, even though she'd tried to get him to do it. She yearned to know more about him.

"Was your dad a farmer, then?"

Jake shook his head.

"I just thought... You said you're from Pennsylvania. And you said he wore overalls..."

"He was a miner," Jake said tonelessly. "At least, he was until he got buried under a few tons of coal."

"Oh, Jake. I'm so sorry."

"No need to be. It was a long time ago."

"It must have been awful for you to lose him."

"Yeah."

Emily heard the world of meaning behind the single word. Her fingers pressed Jake's.

"Losing your father...it must have turned your life upside down."

"Yeah," he said again. Carefully, he withdrew his hand from Emily's, curved it around his coffee cup and lifted the cup to his mouth. "Well, I was just a little kid, you know? But my mother had never thought of herself as anything but a wife. She married the first guy that showed any interest. My stepfather and I...let's just say, he'd signed on for a wife, and the rest was baggage."

"Ah."

"Ah, is right. As soon as I was old enough, I took off."

"For New York?"

"For the army, for Wall Street, for a little of this and that."

"You make it sound easy."

"Life is life, Em. You deal with whatever comes out of the box, that's all."

"Uh-huh." Emily looked at him. "And now you're light-years from the coal mines."

"Light-years, is right." Jake flashed a brittle smile. "Okay."

"Okay, what?"

"Okay, that's my life story. Now, can we get back to talking about other things? The kitchen here turns out an apple pie that—"

"I just wanted to know more about you, that's all."

"Why?"

"What do you mean, why? Because I—because I..."

Emily bit her lip. Whatever she said next would be a mistake. Because I love you? Because I like you? Even that would be disastrous.

She felt her heart break.

She was having an intimate little dinner with her lover, except Jake wasn't her lover. He was her—her instructor. And when had an instructor ever wanted to share his life story with a pupil?

She sat back.

"You're right," she said quietly. "There's no reason for either of us to share the stories of our lives."

Jake's eyebrows rose. "I didn't say that."

"I'm saying it." Emily put her napkin on the table. "It's late. And I really do have to get home."

"Tonight?"

"Tonight."

"But I thought—"

"I know what you thought," she said, with a momentary flash of anger. She could feel her hands shaking and she pushed her plate aside and folded them neatly on the table. There was no reason to be angry. She was the one who'd made all the mistakes. "I know," she said carefully. "You thought we'd spend the night at your house. That we'd make... That we'd sleep together again."

"And you're about to tell me I thought wrong."

There was a cool edge to his words. Oh, Jake, Emily thought, Jake, get out of your chair. Come and pull me into your arms. Tell me you don't just want to sleep with me, that you love me...

"Yes," she said, "as a matter of fact, I am."

There was a long silence. When Jake spoke again, the coolness in his voice had turned to ice.

"In other words, the weekend's over."

"Well, it is. Saturday, Sunday..." Emily forced a smile to her lips. "Tomorrow's Monday, Jake. There's no way to turn back the clock."

Jake's lips tightened. How could she sit there and look at him that way? With eyes as cold as stones on a winter morning, with a polite little smile on her mouth.

He could change that smile, that stony look. All he had to do was take her in his arms and kiss her until she melted with desire, until she begged him to take her, to bury himself within her. Because that was all he was, to her. A damned walking, talking version of the Kama Sutra.

All right. It was what he'd signed on for. And that was fine. It was a relief that she understood that some good sex—okay, some incredible sex—was all that it was.

He wasn't a forever kind of man.

"I'm not interested in turning back the clock," he said. "I just figured we could have a little more fun before the weekend's over."

Fun, Emily thought, and felt the swift, stupid press of tears behind her eyes. Don't you cry, she told herself, don't you dare cry!

"Ah. Well, that would be nice, Jake, but really, I have a lot of work waiting at the office. And you have that trip to San Diego scheduled for tomorrow."

Jake frowned. What was wrong with her? How could she talk about work, how could she look so calm, when he wanted to—when he was going to...

Wait a second. Maybe she figured it was up to her to end things. Maybe she was doing what she figured was the proper thing, after a weekend spent in a man's bed.

"Emily." He reached across the table and caught both of her hands in his. "Listen to me." He gave her the kind of smile he knew always worked on women. "I know this was supposed to be a temporary arrangement but we didn't put a deadline on it. So let's not worry about tomorrow. We'll stay the night, drive back early. As for that trip... I have a great idea. You're my exec, aren't you? Come to California with me.''

Emily felt her heart shatter. And wasn't that stupid? She'd known how this would go. Hadn't she begun the day by telling herself as much? And really, what Jake was suggesting was better than she'd expected. He didn't want to end things immediately. He just wanted to keep a good thing going until he wearied of it.

The bastard.

Emily's chin rose.

Just looking at him made her angry. The sexy smile, the was-it-as-good-for-you-as-it-was-for-me glint in his eyes? And to think she'd been on the verge of tears.

"Sparrow?" He lifted her hand to his mouth and kissed the palm. "Let's not spoil it, hmm?"

"Spoil it?" Emily tugged her hand from his and shoved back her chair. "Spoil such an interesting weekend? I'd never do that."

Jake's smile slipped. "Is that the best you can do? Call this 'an interesting weekend'?"

"I meant it as a compliment. You said you'd teach me to be a woman and you did. I'll always be grateful."

His smile disappeared completely. "What the hell is this?"

"It's my way of saying thank you. For the hair. The clothes. For everything."

She could see him trying to figure out what was happening. No way would he believe she was kissing him off but it was better to be the kisser than the kissee. Something like that, anyway. Her anger was giving way to despair; her heart felt heavy and she knew, oh, she knew, that she'd been too quick to tell herself she wasn't going to cry, too quick to tell herself she hated Jake McBride...

"For everything," she said again, in a bright, cheerful tone. "It was—it was great."

"Great," Jake repeated, his voice low, his features taut, his fingers almost crushing hers.

Why did he have to look at her that way? As if she were hurting him when, dammit, she was the one who was in pain.

"We're finished?" he said. "That's it?"

"Yes. I mean, I really appreciate all you did, Jake—"

"Stop making it sound like an act of charity, goddamn it! I didn't make love to you because it was the right thing to do."

All at once, Emily felt revolted by the part she'd been playing. She was weary, and sick to the depths of her soul. Sick of Jake, of herself, of what had happened.

"Actually," she said shakily, as she pulled her hand free of his, "you didn't make love to me at all."

"Dammit, Emily!"

"Dammit, Jake! Isn't that what you wanted to hear? That what we did this weekend, what you want to keep doing until it gets boring, has nothing to do with making love?"

He glared at her. She was right but hell, there was no reason to lay it out like that. To make things sound so cold-blooded.

Emily shot to her feet. "Don't look so wounded. I know you think every woman over the age of consent is out to put a wedding ring through your nose. Well, I resent you thinking I'm one of them."

Jake stood up, took out his wallet and dropped a handful of bills on the table. Emily had already grabbed her coat and tossed it on; now, she was striding through the place with the other diners in the restaurant doing their best to pretend they weren't watching.

Well, so what? He'd take his time. He'd never run after a woman in his life, especially a crazy one, and he sure wasn't going to start now but, dammit, she was already going to the reservation desk near the door, motioning to the man behind it...

"Emily," Jake shouted, and ran after her. He caught her arm, swung her towards him. "What do you think you're doing?"

"I'm getting a taxi," she said calmly. "This gentleman is—"

"The lady doesn't need a taxi," Jake snarled.

"Don't listen to him." Emily looked at the manager, who was doing his best to become invisible. "I need a ride back to New York."

"Where do you think you are, Em? The Bronx? You can't get a taxi to Manhattan from here."

"I'm afraid the gentleman is right," the manager said nervously. "You can't—"

"You want to go home?" Jake closed his hand around her wrist. "I'll take you home."

"There's no need. I'm perfectly capable of handling this on my own."

"I brought you here. I'll take you back."

He was right. He'd brought her here; he could take her back. Emily nodded stiffly.

"Very well."

Jake marched her out the door, into the parking lot and to his car. She got inside, winced when he slammed the door, and stared straight ahead. The engine roared, the tires slewed sideways on a patch of ice, then squealed as they gained purchase and the car shot out of the parking lot onto the dark road.

Emily looked at the road, then at Jake.

"I don't want to go back to your house. I thought you understood that."

"Neither do I," he said coldly. "But your stuff is there."

"There's nothing of mine at your house."

"Listen," Jake said, his voice humming with tightly repressed fury, "you want to be stupid about us? Okay. Okay, be stupid. But what am I supposed to do with all that clothing, huh? Give it away?"

"There is no 'us.' As for the clothes…save them, for the next woman who walks into your life."

Jake banged his fist on the steering wheel.

"I don't believe this! We spent a weekend together. One weekend, and now you're jealous of somebody who doesn't even exist!"

"But she will!" Emily swung towards him. "She'll exist, and there'll be another one after her and one after that and another and another and another. And you know what? I don't care." Her voice broke, and she took a deep, deep breath. "If you'd only asked me, if you'd said, 'Emily, how do you feel about forever after?' I'd have told you I think it's all hogwash. I'd have said, any woman who thinks love lasts longer than a roller-coaster ride ought to have her head examined. What happens in bed isn't love. People tell themselves it is, well, women do, because they need to make sex sound like—like Mozart."

Jake shot her a look. "What in hell does Mozart have to do with this?"

"That's just my point. He has nothing to do with this. This is all about hormones, and—and random combinations of—of basic animal instincts and—and emotions and—" Emily began to weep.

Thank God, Jake thought frantically. Now, it all made sense. Hormones, instincts, emotions...

He reached across the console and squeezed her knee.

"Baby," he said gently, "you should have told me. Look, if you're approaching that time of the month...if your hormones are going up and down..."

She hit him. Not hard, because she wasn't a complete fool. The night was black, the road slick, and yesterday's near accident had made an impression. But she hit him, nevertheless, a good, solid shot to the arm, delivered with enough power to make him say "oof."

After that there was nothing but merciful silence, all the way through Connecticut, into the city, and to the sidewalk outside her apartment building.

Moments later, Emily was sitting on the floor before Horace's cage, weeping while Horace sang. Ten blocks away,

Jake got pulled over by a policeman who asked, warily, if Jake would like to explain how come he'd gone through the last three red lights in a row.

Jake explained.

"Unbelievable," the cop said when he'd finished, and Jake drove away without a ticket but with the officer's warning that there wasn't a woman in the world worth getting himself killed for...and the assurance that even if there were, no mortal man could possibly hope to understand her.

CHAPTER ELEVEN

JAKE put his car into the garage, rode the elevator to his apartment and stormed inside.

He yanked off his jacket, tossed it in the general vicinity of a chair, headed for the kitchen and switched on the lights.

The room was big, bright, and handsomely done in stark black and white. It was the complete opposite of the kitchen in his Connecticut place, where the walls were old brick and the floor was made of wide-planked wood, although what in hell that had to do with anything was beyond him.

It was just that Emily had made a fuss about the Connecticut kitchen.

"I love this room," she'd said, smiling as she'd fried their eggs this morning, and he'd said yes, it was a terrific room, and then he'd taken her in his arms and kissed her, and found himself wondering what it would be like to spend all the Sundays of his life that way, with coffee on the counter, eggs and bacon on the stove, and Emily in his arms...

Which only went to prove how easily a woman could turn a perfectly intelligent man into a sad, confused ghost of his former self.

Jake opened the refrigerator, took out a bottle of ale and slammed the door shut.

How did women manage these things? How did they put such crazy ideas into a man's head without his even knowing they were doing it? And Emily, of all females...

Unbelievable!

She was the one woman he'd have thought incapable of such witchcraft, but he'd been wrong. The idea hadn't lasted—how could it? But the fact that she'd managed it was terrifying, and never mind her little speech about not wanting forever any more than he did.

"Ha," Jake said as he twisted the cap off the bottle and tossed it into the sink.

They all wanted forever. Nature had hard-wired them that way. Women were nest-builders, plain and simple, but men were meant to fly free—and, dammit, if he came up with one more stupid bird analogy, he was going to explode.

Jake tilted the bottle to his lips and took a long drink.

Women were all the same. Sooner or later, every last one of them brought things down to basics. Man, woman, sex, marriage, and never mind Emily's fancy denials.

Okay, so she'd ended things between them. So she'd made the speech that was usually his, smiled that little smile, said this was it, thank you and goodbye. No more sex. No more laughter. No more walks in the snow or soft little touches, no more sleeping in his arms as if she belonged there after making love.

No. After sex. Because she was right, it was sex, not anything else.

Jake glowered and brought the bottle to his mouth again.

On the other hand, maybe it was a trick. She might have been saying one thing and hoping for another. Why not? No man could ever figure out the twists and turns that the female brain could manage. For all he knew, Emily was sitting by the phone right this minute, waiting for him to call and say, Em, baby, I didn't really want this to end after one weekend or a thousand weekends, I want—I want—

Jake took a swig of ale.

Maybe a monk's cell. Or a padded one. Sanity. Peace and quiet. That was what he wanted. Maybe there was a place out beyond Jupiter where a man could enjoy being with a woman without all these ridiculous complications.

His life was fine, just as it was. Better than fine. He was free. He was doing things he'd never even dreamed of, when he was growing up. In other words, he was happy. Why did women think a man couldn't be happy, unless the poor sap put a ring on her finger and she put a matching one through his nose? Even those who pretended otherwise, thought it. The ones who said they didn't were just lying to themselves...

But Emily hadn't sounded as if she were lying.

Any woman who thinks love lasts longer than a roller-coaster ride ought to have her head examined because what happens in bed isn't love.

Jake took another drink.

That was what she'd said. And it was true. He had always known it. But if Emily believed it, really, honestly believed, as he did, that love was an illusion, why had she gotten so ticked off? When you came down to it, she'd simply told him what he'd already told her, that forever wasn't a viable plan.

Unless—unless it was him she didn't want any part of, not just a relationship that might go on for a while. Hell, he hadn't considered that, the possibility she hadn't liked being with him.

No. Forget that possibility. She had. He knew she had. Those sweet sighs, when they made love. The way she laughed at his jokes, hung onto his every word. The touch of her hand on his, when they were talking...

There'd be no more of that, now. And he'd miss it. All of it, although how he could miss things he'd barely had were beyond him.

So, what was the bottom line here? Why would a woman walk away from an affair when it was still at the hot, electric start?

And "hot" was the word.

Lord, what a weekend. They were perfect together. Better than perfect. Emily was an incredible combination of innocent and sexy.

"Let me," she'd whispered this afternoon, after he'd brought her to release with his mouth. And she'd knelt between his legs, touched him with her tongue, tasted him, pleasured him, and oh, the joy of it, the unbelievable pleasure because sex was different with his sparrow, everything was different, it was—

"Dammit-to-hell!" Jake snarled, and slammed the empty bottle on the counter.

He was wrong. Nothing was different with Emily except, maybe, the way she played the game. Yeah, that was it. She'd lured him on. The shapeless suits. The pulled-back hair. The polite, impersonal way she spoke. "Yes, Mr. McBride." "No, Mr. McBride." Even those horrible personal ads she'd said she was going to answer. It was all part of the game, designed to—

To what?

She'd worked for him for almost a year. And in all that time, she'd never looked at him as if he were a man any more than he'd looked at her as if she was a woman. She hadn't been playing a game. If anyone had been playing games, it was him.

Oh, he'd explained, told her he was going to help her change into a woman men would desire but, in the end, he was the man who'd desired her.

Now, she could go out and practice what he'd taught her with someone else.

Jake felt as if a hand had torn open his chest and ripped out his heart.

His Emily, with another man?

No. No, he couldn't let that happen. He wanted—he wanted...

He didn't know what he wanted, and it was all Emily's fault. She'd taken a perfectly simple thing, a weekend in bed, and turned it into an equation as complex as quantum mechanics.

Jake's jaw tightened. He switched off the kitchen light, strode into his bedroom, and got undressed.

He would tell her that, tomorrow morning. He had that

California meeting but no way was he going to fly west until this was settled.

"Emily," he'd say, "you overreacted. But because you're new to all this, I'm going to give you another chance. We'll forget all about that nasty little scene Sunday night. We can pretend it never happened..."

And if she laughed in his face, then what?

Jake got into bed, folded his hands beneath his head and stared into the darkness.

He could fire her. That was what.

He switched off the light, rolled on his belly and pummeled his pillow into shape.

Half an hour later, he switched the light on, folded his hands under his head again and glared at the ceiling.

He wouldn't fire her. How could he, when that was probably exactly what she expected so she could call him a vindictive bastard on top of everything else?

Anyway, it wouldn't come to that. She wouldn't laugh when he offered her the chance to turn back the clock. She'd go into his arms, kiss him, and just that easily, they'd agree to keep the office business in the office and the bedroom business where it belonged.

Jake smiled.

He knew, in his heart, that was what Emily really wanted. It was just that women were such emotional creatures. Not that he'd say so. Hell, that comment he'd made, about hormones and the time of the month...

"You were just asking for trouble, pal," he muttered.

Still, it was true. Female feelings gyrated like the stock market on a really bad day. Victims of emotion, all of them, even Emily. Really, what would women do without men to ensure that the world remained a logical place?

Okay. He had it all sorted out. Go to San Diego tomorrow, come back on Tuesday, don't phone her or do anything until he saw her at the office on Wednesday. Give her lots of time to think about the mistake she'd made. Keep her worrying, even turn panicky when she realized how much she missed him...

Yes, indeed.

When he turned out the light, Jake McBride fell into a deep, dreamless sleep.

The snow that had blanketed Connecticut had left the city of Rochester untouched, which was a rare event because, growing up, Emily had thought of her hometown as the Snow Capital of the Universe.

She thought of that now, as she began preparing dinner for her sisters in the house the two of them shared, and wasn't it great that it wasn't snowing?

Coming back to the place you thought you'd escaped, having to ask your sisters if you might stay with them for a while, was difficult enough. Doing it while the city was trapped under an inverted white bowl would have made it seem twice as dreary.

Not that she didn't like Rochester. Her roots were here, and her family. Of course, her parents didn't know she was back. Not yet. She'd wait, give herself time to find a job, an apartment and, most of all, a logical excuse for coming home.

She didn't want her mother looking at her father with her eyebrows raised, the way Serena had looked at Angela when she'd arrived on their doorstep with a bird, a birdcage, and three big suitcases Monday evening.

"Hi," she'd said brightly. "Can I move in with you guys for a while?"

"Of course," her sisters had said, and then they'd looked at each other, and she'd read all the questions in their faces but they were her sisters, and it was okay to look right back and tell them there wasn't a way in the world she was going to answer any questions.

Emily sighed.

She'd never imagined coming back for anything but a visit.

She'd had such big plans when she left for New York all those years ago. An exciting career, in an exciting city…

Emily blew a curl off her forehead, opened the oven door and checked on the meat loaf baking inside.

And she'd had that, until she'd ruined it all.

The sad thing was that she'd never thought about having a man in her life, except in the most casual way, until she'd gone to work for Jake. And then, as the months passed, she'd begun to wonder if she wasn't missing some-thing…something like her tall, dark and handsome boss, who often visited her in her dreams.

Strange, how she'd never admitted that to herself until Sunday night, when she'd done nothing but dream of Jake. Of course, those dreams had been different. She'd buried him alive in a snowbank, in one dream. And she'd chained him to his bed and fed him cephalopod mollusks until he begged for mercy in another.

Emily slammed the oven door, went to the pantry and took out an onion and some potatoes.

So much for dreams, and so much for Jake. She was home and happy to be here. Rochester was a big place. She'd find a good job, a great apartment, and she'd never waste another second of her life, thinking about Jacob McBride.

She'd already wasted a lot of tears on him, and for what? The thing they'd done, the bedroom business, had been noth-ing but an aberration. It had taken her all of Monday to re-alize it, but that was all it was.

Her heart, thank goodness, was intact.

Serena and Angela didn't think so.

"It's a man," they'd kept saying. "It has to be, Emily. You fell in love and he broke your heart. That's why you ran away."

And finally Emily had admitted that yes, there'd been a man, but she hadn't fallen in love and she hadn't run away.

"I just got tired of New York, that's all. Nobody broke my heart."

Certainly not, she thought as she peeled the onion and diced it. Just because she'd packed her things, sold her furniture to the superintendent, arranged to have her books, her CDs and some other stuff packed and shipped, and put herself and Horace on a train all in one day, didn't mean she'd run away.

A tear ran down her cheek. "Damned onions," she muttered, and wiped the dampness away with her apron.

She had not run. Why would she? She had ended her relationship with Jake, if you could call a night a relationship. Then, after she'd thought it over, she'd decided a preemptive strike made sense. So she'd quit, before he could have the satisfaction of firing her, quit without notice or warning and left him in the lurch.

It was a great feeling.

Emily smiled tightly as she peeled the potatoes and cut them in quarters.

Oh, if only she could see the look on his handsome face when he came into the office Wednesday and found her gone. No Emily to make his appointments. Type his letters. Keep his files. No Emily to make his coffee, take his dictation, organize his notes...

Lie in his arms.

She frowned, took out a pot, dumped the potatoes in and filled it with water.

Where had that silly thought come from? Jake would hardly notice. He'd have some other woman in his arms before the week ended. Yes, maybe she'd dented his ego a little because he was the one who was supposed to end things.

After all, he was the Great Jake McBride.

"Great Egotistical Jerk, is more like it," she muttered, as she put the pot on the stove and turned on the burner.

Did he think every woman he bedded really wanted to spend the rest of her life with him?

"Ha," Emily said.

She didn't want to spend her life with any male, except

for Horace. As for that nonsense she'd spun in her head, that she'd fallen in love with Jake...

"Ha," she said again, and Horace chirped and fluttered his wings as if he found the idea as preposterous as she did. She didn't love Jake. It was just sex that had made her think so. All those shooting stars going off...

Yes, the sex had been terrific. But love?

"No way," she muttered, but the conviction in her head didn't connect with the anguish in her heart and, dammit, there she was, crying again. It was ridiculous. She'd been weeping, on and off, since Sunday night, which was why Serena and Angela kept exchanging those looks...

"Who is he?" Serena had asked, just this morning.

"Probably some fast-talking used-car salesman like the one I divorced," Angela had said, answering the question when Emily wouldn't.

"No," Serena had replied, "he's probably a duplicate of the skirt-chasing SOB I got rid of." Then she'd put her arm around Emily and hugged her. "Sweetie, what can we tell you? Men are all the same. Even the ones who look like pet mice are only rats in disguise."

"Jake doesn't look like a pet anything," Emily had said, her voice wobbling, "but you're right, he's a grade A, 100% rat."

And he was.

Emily yanked a paper towel from the roll, wiped her eyes and blew her nose.

This was ridiculous. She had not, repeat, not, loved Jake. Why would she? He was gorgeous and sexy and fun to be with but he wasn't the lovable kind.

If she cried, it was over her own foolishness in falling for him. In *thinking* she'd fallen for him, because she hadn't. She hadn't. She—

"Emily? I'm ho-ome."

Emily blew her nose again and tried, unsuccessfully, to tuck her hair behind her ears.

Angela was here. That meant Serena would be coming in, too, in just a few minutes. And she wasn't going to have either of them sneak little looks at her, or at each other, anymore. The very last thing she needed right now was to have her two beautiful sisters feeling sorry for her. She'd had enough of that in high school to last a lifetime.

"There you are, Emily." Angela, looking elegant as always, her blond hair shiny and smooth, her blue eyes sparkling, slipped an arm around Emily's waist and hugged her. "Mmm. Something smells good."

"Meat loaf," Emily said, and felt two gigantic tears trickle down her cheeks.

"Oh, Em." Angela sighed and put her hands on Emily's shoulders. "Sweetie, don't! Whoever he is, he's not worth it."

Emily nodded and wiped her eyes. "You're right," she said briskly. "And—and I'm not crying. I was—I was chopping onions."

"Onions?" Serena said, as she entered the kitchen. "Great. I don't have a date tonight, so…" She bit her lip, shot a guilty look at Emily. "I mean, I adore onions. And what's that luscious smell?"

"Meat loaf," Angela said, and shot a warning look at her sister.

Serena raised her eyebrows. "What? I like meat loaf. I wouldn't say anything bad about meat…" She looked at Emily. "Oh, Emily. Sweetie, you're crying."

"I am not crying. What's with you two? Don't you know onion tears when you see them?"

Serena turned her crystalline blue gaze on Emily, put an arm around her and hugged her. Strands of perfectly groomed, dark gold hair brushed Emily's cheek.

"You have to believe us," she said firmly. "Whoever he is, he's not worth it."

"For heaven's sake, I am not crying about a man. Can't you two get that straight?"

"You've been crying since you got here," Angela said sternly. "And just look at what it's done to you. Serena, have you ever seen a redder nose? And those swollen eyes, all red-ringed. Honestly, Emily..."

"Honestly, Angela," Emily said, with a little laugh, "I hoped you'd appreciate the fact that I'm color-coordinated. Red nose, red eyes..." She waited for her sisters to smile, but they didn't. "Oh, come on, guys. Lighten up. After all, it's just like old times, right? You're portraits of perfection. And I'm a mess."

Angela and Serena, each three swanlike inches taller than Emily, exchanged looks over her head.

"You don't have to be," Serena said gently. "You could use my cucumber pads on your eyes. And I have a cream that would do wonders for your nose."

"Yes," Angela said, just as gently. "Emily, you know, looking better would make you feel better."

Emily sighed. "I don't think so."

"Oh, it would. I mean, just look at what you're wearing. Baggy old jeans. A ratty sweatshirt. And your hair..."

"Would you believe I had it cut and styled on Saturday, by a guy who styles the hair of half the models in New York?"

"No," her sisters said, with one voice.

Emily put on a pair of mitts, opened the oven and peered at the meat loaf.

"Well, I did. And his hair was blonder and longer than yours."

"Now, Emily..."

"Look, both of you." Emily took a deep breath. "I know you mean well. But I have to work this out for myself."

Angela and Serena exchanged looks again. "Ah-ha."

Emily yanked off the oven mitts. "Okay. So I ran away. Well, you would have, too. I made the mistake of getting involved with a no-good rat. A fast-talking, lying, cheating, miserable rat who—who—"

"They're all liars, and fast-talking rats," said Angela.

"Yes," Serena said. "And they cheat, too."

Tears rose in Emily's eyes again. "He didn't cheat," she said miserably. "He didn't lie, either. That's the problem. He told me, straight out, that he wasn't the forever kind. That he just wanted me for—for sex."

"I never, ever said that, Sparrow," a man's voice said.

Emily, Angela and Serena all spun around. Emily's eyes widened with shock. Angela's and Serena's eyes widened, too, but not with shock.

"Jake?" Emily whispered.

"You're damned right, it's Jake," Jake said coldly. "And you're lucky it is. What's the matter with you women? You think you can just leave doors open and only the good fairy will take you up on the invitation?"

Angela looked at Serena, who blushed. "I forgot. I wore boots, because it was supposed to snow, and I took them off outside…"

"Jake?" Emily said again. Her heart felt as if it were trying to leap out of her chest. She put her hand over it, as if that might slow its race. "Jake, what are you doing here?"

Jake stared at Emily. What *was* he doing here? He'd had a speech all planned, about how she'd scared the hell out of him by running off like that, about how he was totally and completely ticked off, that a really good executive assistant would never do such a thing…but now that he was here, he was tongue-tied.

Well, no wonder. What time zone was this, anyway? What day? What year? Yesterday, he'd been in California, sitting through a meeting with all the attentiveness of a chimpanzee at a ballet. People were spouting facts and numbers like hyperactive geysers but the only thing he could think of was what would happen to him if he lost Emily.

Eventually, he'd excused himself to the bewildered CEO, gone into the hall, pulled out his cell phone and called her. He'd tried to, anyway. But she didn't answer the phone in the office and when he called her at home, he got a recorded voice that said the number had been disconnected.

The panic he'd felt had made his blood run cold.

He'd gone back to the meeting, made some halfhearted excuse, headed for the airport and paced the first class lounge and dialed Emily's apartment and his office until the battery on his cell phone died.

While he paced, he came up with half a dozen scenarios to explain her absence, each one worse than the last.

The only thing he knew for certain was that his Emily, his sweet little sparrow, his impossible, pigheaded sparrow, had disappeared from his life.

How would he find her? Detectives? Private investigators? The police?

At last, he'd boarded a plane. And halfway over the country, the solution had come to him. He had Mrs. Levy's name. He had her address. He had an inflight phone...

"Jake? I asked you a question. How did you find me?"

"Mrs. Levy told me."

Emily felt behind her for a chair. Her legs were wobbly. Jake looked so angry. So enraged.

So handsome.

Oh, so handsome. And so disheveled. He'd tossed his overcoat on a chair, undone his jacket, loosened his tie. He kept running his hands through his hair so that it lay in heavy waves against his forehead. He hadn't shaved, either; his jaw was stubbled and with what she knew was painfully bad timing, she remembered how it had felt that first time he'd made love to her, when his stubbled jaw had rubbed against her skin. Against her breasts...

Color shot into her face.

Angela noticed. "Oh, my," she whispered. "Serena?"

"Yes." Serena licked her lips. "Emily? Is this the man?"

"No," Emily said. She took a deep breath and lifted her chin. "He's not *the* man. He's just a man."

"Oh, but he's gorgeous," Serena said softly. "Isn't he, Ange?"

Jake narrowed his eyes. "Who are these women, Emily?"

"My—my sisters." Her beautiful sisters, who were all but drooling. Well, Jake would drool, too, once he took a good, long look at them. "This is Serena. And Angela."

"Hi," Angela cooed, and smiled.

"Hello," Serena hummed, and smiled.

Jake looked at each of them. "Hello," he said, and scowled. "Now would the two of you please get the hell out of here and give us some privacy?"

Emily blinked. Serena and Angela did, too, but then they laughed, kissed Emily, one on each cheek, and did exactly as Jake had commanded.

Emily stared at him.

"You—you just told my sisters to go away."

"Damned right, I did."

"But—but they're beautiful."

"Are they?" Jake shrugged his shoulders and started towards her. "I didn't notice."

"What do you mean, you didn't notice? You have to notice. Serena and Angela are—they are... Jake. Jake, what are you doing?"

"Kissing you," Jake said, as he threaded his hands into Emily's hair and tilted her face to his.

And he did. Oh, he did. Not gently. Not politely. His mouth covered hers and he kissed her with all the hunger that he'd kept locked within his lonely, hungry soul.

Emily told herself not to respond. There was no reason to, because this was only sex. It was only sex...

It was sex, and it was love, for her, anyway, because the man holding her in his arms was all she had ever wanted.

After a long time, Jake drew back.

"Dammit," he said huskily, "I am furious at you, Sparrow." He proved it by kissing her again. "I ought to turn you over my knee and spank you."

"Kiss me instead," Emily whispered, and he did. Eventually, she pushed gently against his chest. "Jake," she said softly, "you came after me."

"Of course I came after you! Did you think I was the kind of man you could walk out on? The kind who'd let you go without a fight?" He drew a deep breath. "I won't let you leave me."

Emily hesitated, but not for long. She rose on her toes, clasped Jake's face and kissed him. It was, she knew, what a real woman would do, what she'd have the courage to do, if she loved a man.

And she loved Jake. She'd always love him, and she was woman enough, too, to accept whatever he offered, for as long as he offered it. Besides, miracles could happen. Jake might change. He might fall in love with her.

The risk was terrifying, but risk was what made life worth living. She knew that, now.

Emily smiled. "I won't leave you. I thought I had to, but I was wrong."

Jake kissed her again, over and over. He couldn't get enough of her taste, her sweetness, of the way she fit so perfectly into his arms, and into his heart.

"Sparrow." He pulled back, just a little. "Sparrow, you were wrong."

"I know. I just said so. I shouldn't have—"

"I *am* a forever kind of guy. And you're a forever kind of woman. We just needed to find the right person to be forever with." Jake gave a soft laugh. "I'm making a mess of this. I was going to do it perfectly, say it poetically..."

"Say what?" Emily said carefully, because it was too much to hope for.

Jake took a deep breath. "I love you, Em. I love you with all my heart, and you'd damn well better tell me you love me, too, and that you really do believe in forever because if you don't..." He stopped and looked deep into her eyes. "If you don't," he said softly, "I'll be lost and lonely, for the rest of my life.'' He lifted her face to his. "Em? Tell me you love me, too.''

Emily wanted to laugh. She wanted to cry. Instead, she kissed Jake's mouth.

"Of course I love you. And I believe in forever, so long as it's with you.''

Jake grinned. "The only things I don't believe in,'' he said, "are long engagements.''

Emily laughed. Jake did, too, and he drew her close and kissed her. She kissed him back. Horace, observing all this, burst into song.

Beyond the kitchen, in the living room, Serena and Angela sighed, smiled tearily at each other, slipped into their coats and tiptoed out the door.

VIVA LA VIDA DE AMOR!

They speak the language of passion.

In Harlequin Presents®, you'll find a special
kind of lover—full of Latin charm. Whether
he's relaxing in denims or dressed for dinner,
giving you diamonds or simply sweet dreams,
he's got spirit, style and sex appeal!

Latin Lovers is the new miniseries
from Harlequin Presents® for anyone
who enjoys hot romance!

Meet gorgeous Antonio Scarlatti in
THE BLACKMAILED BRIDEGROOM
by Miranda Lee, Harlequin Presents® #2151
available January 2001

And don't miss sexy Niccolo Dominici in
THE ITALIAN GROOM
by Jane Porter, Harlequin Presents® #2168
available March 2001!

Available wherever Harlequin books are sold.

HARLEQUIN Presents
Passion™

Looking for stories that **sizzle?**

Wanting a read that has a little extra **spice?**

Harlequin Presents® is thrilled to bring you romances that turn up the **heat!**

Every other month there'll be a
PRESENTS PASSION™
book by one of your favorite authors.

Don't miss
THE BEDROOM BUSINESS
by **Sandra Marton**

On sale February 2001, Harlequin Presents® #2159

Pick up a **PRESENTS PASSION™** novel—
where **seduction** is guaranteed!

Available wherever Harlequin books are sold.

HARLEQUIN®
Makes any time special ™

He's a man of cool sophistication.
He's got pride, power and wealth.
He's a ruthless businessman, an expert lover—
and he's one hundred percent committed
to staying single.

Until now. Because suddenly he's responsible
for a BABY!

HIS BABY

An exciting miniseries from Harlequin Presents®
He's sexy, he's successful...
and now he's facing up to fatherhood!

On sale February 2001:
RAFAEL'S LOVE-CHILD
by Kate Walker, Harlequin Presents® #2160

On sale May 2001:
MORGAN'S SECRET SON
by Sara Wood, Harlequin Presents® #2180

And look out for more later in the year!

Available wherever Harlequin books are sold.

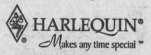

#1 *New York Times* bestselling author

NORA ROBERTS

brings you more of the loyal and loving, tempestuous and tantalizing Stanislaski family.

Coming in February 2001

The Stanislaski Sisters

Natasha and Rachel

Though raised in the Old World traditions of their family, fiery Natasha Stanislaski and cool, classy Rachel Stanislaski are ready for a *new* world of love....

And also available in February 2001 from Silhouette Special Edition, the newest book in the heartwarming Stanislaski saga

CONSIDERING KATE

Natasha and Spencer Kimball's daughter Kate turns her back on old dreams and returns to her hometown, where she finds the *man* of her dreams.

Available at your favorite retail outlet.

Silhouette®

™ *Where love comes alive*™

In March 2001,

Silhouette® Desire®

presents the next book in

DIANA PALMER's

enthralling *Soldiers of Fortune* trilogy:

THE WINTER SOLDIER

Cy Parks had a reputation around Jacobsville for his
taciturn and solitary ways. But spirited Lisa Monroe
wasn't put off by the mesmerizing mercenary, and drove
him to distraction with her sweetly tantalizing kisses.
Though he'd never admit it, Cy was getting mighty
possessive of the enchanting woman who needed the
type of safeguarding only he could provide. But who
would protect the beguiling beauty from *him...?*

Soldiers of Fortune...prisoners of love.

Silhouette®

Where love comes alive™

*Available only from
Silhouette Desire at
your favorite retail outlet.*

Visit Silhouette at
www.eHarlequin.com

SDWS

If you enjoyed what you just read,
then we've got an offer you can't resist!

Take 2 bestselling
love stories FREE!
Plus get a FREE surprise gift!

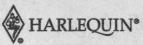